ESCAPE

EMMA EGGLESTON

CONTENTS

LAILA'S ACKNOWLEDGMENTS

Dear reader,

I have always wanted to be a writer, to tell stories, to create things, and to inspire people.

There was a time in my life when this seemed entirely possible. I had belief and everything seemed so worth writing down.

Then, I met somebody who changed my life completely and he gave me more reason to write than ever. I wanted to write because I felt his stories deserved to be told, but I also wrote because I wanted to remember everything about him.

And just as this somebody came into my life unexpectedly, so he left it. I didn't want to write anymore with him gone. It hurt too much for a long time, but every day I recalled happy memories of this person so that when I was ready to write again, I wouldn't have forgotten a thing.

Finally, the day came when it was okay to write again. I found everything I had written before and then I wrote some more. I asked questions of others. I begged them to help me get the story right and they did.

The result is the book you hold in your hands. It's the story of when Matty Holt and Laila Jennings collided together and they traveled to surreal places feeling more alive than they ever had. It's a story of love, of sadness, of joy, and of hope. Now, I'm giving it to you. I hope this story makes you a better person like it did me.

I have to thank my parents for teaching me the importance of art, my children for being my drive, my husband for helping me to draft and publish this book, and my best friend, Matty for being the subject of it.

Lastly, I want to thank you for taking a chance on a new author.

Much love,

Laila Jennings Stewart

1 LAILA

"Laila Jennings," the teacher called from her spot in the front of the classroom.

"Laila Jennings," she called out yet again. This time the frustration was evident in her voice. She did not like having to repeat herself.

But the seventeen-year-old girl still did not answer. Not out of rudeness or disobedience, but simply because she did not hear her teacher's calls.

Laila was lost in a daydream. While her classmates willed themselves to take notes on Keynesian economics, Laila gave in to her persistent imagination and instead was penning poetry about what it might feel like to leave her hometown of Richardsville, Pennsylvania.

It wasn't like Laila was terribly desperate to leave the only place she had ever lived. No, she was not one of those ungrateful high school seniors who called their town lame every day for eight months only to find themselves waiting tables at the town's run-down diner six months after graduation. In fact, there were things she found objectively charming about Richardsville.

Laila thought the flower garden in the center of the public park was the loveliest place to sit on a balmy spring day with a good book and the whisper of the babbling brook in the background. Laila liked the sound of cargo trains rushing by every day on the tracks that split the town into two sides. She loved the Amish people with their curious old-fashioned looking apparel and vast, green farms from which her mother bought produce every weekend. And of course, Laila liked that it was small and quiet because she was a small and quiet girl.

However, being the sort-of misfit girl she was, there were certain things she did not appreciate about Richardsville.

For example, the town lacked art enough to satisfy her existential and creative mind. There were no galleries to peruse paintings, no theatres to put on plays, and no large stages where musicians would come and perform.

Another thing that troubled Laila about her hometown was that there was no one to really talk to. Sure, Laila could have joined her fellow schoolgirls in the gossip they shared every day for the past six years, but she didn't want to.

Laila didn't refuse to join in the rumor-spreading because she was morally better than her counterparts, but rather because she was much more interested in herself and her thoughts than the weekly break-ups and make-ups.

What Laila truly desired was someone to listen to her thoughts on hot-button topics and someone who might have important things to say back to her.

Laila tried her best to find someone to have those important conversations with her that was so rarely heard around high school cafeteria tables.

Although the girl was surely an introvert she didn't mind introducing herself to others. Laila found people very interesting and enjoyed getting to know new ones.

Throughout her three and a half years as a student at Richardsville High School, Laila had joined everything from marching band to academic decathlon. She met some companions who made lunch hours and hallway passings more tolerable, but she never found anyone to invite over to spend the night or to whisper secrets to before class.

By age sixteen, Laila realized that to deeply know and be known was not an experience she would have while this small town was her world.

Alternatively, Laila leaned into her long-time loves of reading books until early in the morning, listening to music no one else cared for, and escaping into daydreams or creative activities whenever a fascinating thought passed through her mind.

The compulsion to daydream was irresistible and a source of great comfort to Laila as it is to anyone who feels like they don't fit in. However, it was quite inconvenient to her learning when she found herself lost in thought during the middle of an important lecture or class discussion as she had in Ms. Fredericks class that day.

Laila was jolted back into reality by a tap on her shoulder from the boy seated behind her. She looked around and noticed that the entire class was looking in one of three places, at their notes, at Ms. Fredericks, or worst of all at her.

Laila felt her cheeks turn red. This was a situation she had been in before, being called on while not paying attention, but that didn't make it any less embarrassing.

"I'm sorry, Ms. Fredericks, what was that?" the girl asked hurriedly.

The teacher subtly shifted her weight from one side to another as an expression of her disapproval.

"Please, read back your notes for the class, Laila," the woman instructed in a monotone voice.

"Oh, yes," Laila nodded while on the inside she panicked.

Ms. Fredericks always asked one student to give a summary of their notes at the end of class, but of course, Laila had no notes to give a summary of.

"I'm sorry, my notes, they, um… I'm having a hard time making sense of them," Laila mumbled. She hoped the teacher would skip over her, but instead Ms. Fredericks kept her gaze steady on Laila.

"Just read what you have written. I saw you scribbling during the lecture. You must have something down." At this point, some of Laila's classmates began to giggle, smirk, or catch glances with each other.

Laila's heart rate quickened and her hands perspired. Laila didn't know what to say so she sat staring down at her notebook wishing she could sink into the floor.

Ms. Fredericks walked to the third row where Laila sat. Her cream-colored kitten heels clicked with each step. When she stopped by Laila, the girl looked up at her teacher with a blank face and then back down at the words in her spiral-bound notebook.

Laila wondered if the middle-aged woman got a thrill from embarrassing her.

Laila watched the older woman's eyes in anticipation as they moved back and forth reading each word of the girl's poem. Most of the students had lost interest in the charade now. They had all seen it before, but today something different was going to happen.

"Read it," Ms. Fredericks commanded softly, but firmly.

"The poem?" Laila asked terrified hoping she had misheard her teacher's order.

Ms. Fredericks was impatient so instead of a verbal answer, she gave a clear and visible nod. Laila hesitated for a moment. If she waited for a second, she thought maybe she would wake up from the bad dream, but after a moment's pause, she accepted her reality.

The girl took a deep breath, coughed briefly and unnecessarily, then steadied her eyes on the first line of her poem. In a low, but clear voice she read the words as she had written them.

Little town I can picture you now
White picket fences
Perfect lawns
Lots of trees
Little town where I used to run and hide
Now it seems you're hiding from me

Little school I still hear your bells toll
Books and pencils
Late for class
Best friends that wouldn't last
Little school where I was never that cool
It seems I'm much bigger than you now

Little house I'm sleeping on your couch
Flowered sheets
Wooden swing
Doggy door
Little house I don't belong here anymore

But I'm not ready to walk out the door

I packed my bags and left for the big city
Full of dreams and hopes I'd never see-through
And so I came back to you
But somehow you weren't there
Little town where have you gone?

Where do you go when your town is gone?
What do you do when your home's not sweet?
I guess I've got to move on

Much to Ms. Fredericks's surprise, the class was quiet and respectful while Laila read her poem. Ms. Fredericks was slightly disappointed in this. She had wanted the student to be more humiliated, but instead, there seemed to be an unspoken admiration for Laila's art amongst her peers. It was something Ms. Fredericks had never seen in her twenty-two years of teaching. Usually, even the oldest of students were cruel and teased each other whenever the opportunity arrived.

Laila continued to look down at the words on her paper after she had read them. She was glad that her classmates hadn't jeered or laughed. She assumed that they too had a dislike for Ms. Fredericks and didn't want to give her the satisfaction of making a student feel poorly.

For a moment, there was silence in the room after Laila had finished speaking. Then the teacher spoke, "Please take notes on the subject matter next class, Miss Jennings."

Laila nodded in a sullen agreement and then the bell rang. It was the end of the school day, so although Ms. Fredericks had not formally dismissed them; the students started chatting and packing up their belongings.

The unhappy teacher thought about admonishing the class, but she was too tired and knew that she didn't stand a chance against all twenty-five of their chattering voices and zipping of book bags. Instead, she walked to her standard teacher's desk in the back of the classroom and secretively unlocked the bottom left-hand drawer. Inside was six ounces of whiskey she had been saving for a very stressful day. Once the last student was out of the classroom, she would take a long swig.

Laila left the classroom and walked down the stairs until she reached the ground floor. She looked down at her feet the whole time hoping not to run into anybody who had been in her economics class. All she wanted to do was go home, be alone in her room, and listen to the *Abbey Road* record her father had given her for her fifteenth birthday.

Laila breathed in a deep sigh of relief once she had made it out the doors of the red-brick school building. She had made it out without having to make awkward, embarrassing eye contact with any of her classmates and so she was happy.

Laila pushed the afternoon's events out of her mind. They were embarrassing, but they were in the past and so she chose not to dwell on them. That had been something her grandmother taught her to do since she was a little girl. "Leave the past in the past and live in the present," she would tell her granddaughter as they baked chocolate chip cookies together or planted bulbs in her flower garden.

The teenage girl in her coat, gloves, and hat looked around at every house and every tree she passed on the three-block journey from her high school to her home and looked for something unique or interesting about it.

She noticed how the two-story on the corner of Spring St. and Forest Ave. had put up precisely fifteen blow-up Christmas figures including an elf this year which was new. She admired the poinsettia flowers in the old widow's ranch a few houses down from her own. Most of all, she liked the way the snow looked different on every tree it fell upon.

Laila's life was not always fun. Sometimes it was the opposite of fun, but Laila believed that even if things weren't fun they could still be beautiful and so that's how she saw the world.

2 MATTY

Matty was popular. It wasn't difficult to figure out why. The boy, who was days away from his eighteenth birthday, had everything other people wanted.

He was smart, but not in a know-it-all kind of way. Matty studied to please his "Type A" parents who married after meeting in law school, but he didn't have to work as hard as some of his peers because he was born highly intelligent. He would be accepted into every college he applied to.

In addition to being clever, he was also athletic and good-looking. As a member of the soccer team and as track-and-field captain, Matty was fit and toned, but not overly muscular. His hair was thick and dark brown, the same color as his eyes. Matty's face still had a distinct boyishness to it, but his jawline was defined and sharp. He had been the recipient of many adoring giggles, stares, and whispers from his female classmates since around the time he turned thirteen. He almost always ignored them.

The thing about Matty that probably made him so likable was his smile. Matty's teeth and lips were nice, but what made Matty's grin so entrancing was the sincerity of it and the warmth behind it. When Matty smiled at someone, they felt like he was embracing them in a big bear hug and telling them that everything was going to be okay.

What nobody knew about Matty's smile was the irony of it. Matty loved to make others happy and so he dutifully smiled and laughed with each person he met. Afterward, whoever had conversed with Matty would usually walk away standing a little taller and feeling more optimistic than they had before, but Matty would feel the same sadness he felt every day.

Matty had what most people would consider an ideal childhood. He grew up in a pleasant American small-town. His mother gave birth to him when she and his father were in their early thirties. Both his parents were educated, financially stable, and loving.

He lived in the same large house since the day he was taken home from the hospital. He was an only child but always had the companionship of cousins, teammates, and school friends to bide his time. His family attended Richardsville 1st Methodist Church where he participated in Christmas pageants and summer camps until his teen years.

Matty had no reason to be unhappy, but for some reason, at fourteen years old he began to feel depressed.

It started slow for Matty. He didn't feel as hungry at mealtimes as he usually did and he felt a little extra tired. Matty couldn't understand why but he forced himself not to think about it. He was too busy training to become Richardsville's hometown hero to get caught up in such things.

Then, a couple of weeks passed and Matty started doing something he had seldom done since he was a little boy. He cried.

The first time he cried was on Monday when he found out he had gotten C's on two of his history assignments. He thought to himself that it shouldn't bother him, but it did. When he came home from school that afternoon, Matty went up to his bedroom, collapsed on his bed, and cried into his pillowcase.

Matty felt so ashamed for crying even though it was in the privacy of his bedroom and his parents weren't yet home from work to hear him.

Matty believed that boys weren't supposed to cry, at least not audibly and for as long as he had. Perhaps, a few tears with the passing of a close loved one was acceptable, but a boy crying for receiving poor marks was inappropriate.

The worst part of all for the ninth-grader was that he couldn't understand why he was feeling so upset. Bad grades were unusual for him, but not unheard of. He had gotten C's before and even a few D's on assignments in the past and it hadn't bothered him like

8

this.

Because Matty felt his feelings were illogical and because he wanted to be a "man" like his father and uncles, Matty resolved to hide what was going on inside of him from everyone, even his sweet mother who he was, especially close to.

Matty assumed that eventually, the unexplainable feelings would vanish, but he was wrong. Over the next six months, things got worse instead of better. The feelings he had of sadness and loneliness turned into dangerous thoughts and showed up at the most inconvenient times like on the end-of-the-year class trip to the amusement park.

Matty liked most rides and rollercoasters except for the SkyDrop. That was the one ride he wouldn't go on, but of course, all of his friends wanted him to ride it with them.

"Come on, Matty. It'll be fun," his pal, Finn, had teased him good-naturedly.

"Yeah, Holt! Don't be a wimp," another chuckled playfully.

Matty had succumbed to peer pressure before on instances of party games like Truth or Dare, but he was not giving in this time.

"No," he said kindly but without leaving room for argument, "you guys go on though. Have fun. I'll just wait over here on this bench."

His friends shrugged in defeat, assured Matty that they would be back soon, and then rushed, laughing toward the ride. Matty sat down. He felt alone sitting on the park bench watching as a group of girls from his class walked by taking selfies with their cotton candy.

"I don't fit in," Matty thought consciously for the first time. It wasn't true, of course. His friends would be back in a matter of minutes and they would want to hang out with him because they liked him, but Matty didn't think that or believe that.

As a hot wave of anxiety swept through his body, Matty began to think about all the reasons why he didn't deserve friendship. He remembered the time he had lost the soccer game for his team by missing a crucial shot. He remembered when he had messed up reading the opening prayer at church. He remembered that his teeth weren't perfectly straight and that he had an unusual red birthmark on his arm.

It was then, in those fifteen minutes of innocent waiting that

Matty first started to dislike himself and to believe that he was a loser.

His friends greeted him cheerfully when they returned from the ride. Matty put on his smile and pretended like everything was perfectly fine. The crew of freshmen boys then agreed to stop for ice cream. Matty spent the rest of the day going along with them, riding bumper cars, posing in silly ways for the photograph on the water flume, and convincing everyone that he was having fun.

But on the inside Matty was miserable. He wanted to go home and be alone. His heart felt constantly heavy from the sadness that weighed upon it. Matty felt real pain, but he was a good actor and so his best friends, Finn, Colin, and Jake were completely unsuspecting.

Soon after the trip, Matty's freshman year came to an unceremonious end. He was glad too because acting like he was happy every day, when he wasn't, was wearing him down. At the same time, Matty was not as excited about summer vacation as he had been in previous years.

The days of jumping into swimming pools, riding bicycles, and catching fireflies without a care in the world seemed long gone from him now.

Matty felt a little better after a few weeks of sitting alone in the sunshine and taking long walks on the mountainside behind his home. The constant pressure to perform academically and athletically was relieved at least for a little while.

However, there were still things that bothered him like when he woke up in the morning, looked in the mirror, and saw one too many pimples on his face. Or when thought about the girl he liked with the red hair and the handsome, older boyfriend popped into his head.

Then, there were the thoughts about the future and the past that would come into his mind and upset him. Matty had a bad habit of lying in bed at night and replaying every embarrassing incident or failure he had had in his fifteen years until he was so worked up he would have to go downstairs and run on the treadmill until he was so tired, he couldn't keep his eyes open any longer.

While trivial regrets of the past haunted him at night, the mention of college, a career, or a girlfriend was enough to send Matty into a flurry of worry and anxiety. Like most kids his age, he didn't know what he wanted to do with his life.

He hadn't a clue where or what he wanted to study after high school. He worried that he wouldn't ever know and would end up doing something he hated for the rest of his life.

Matty also felt behind his peers in that he had never had a girlfriend or even gone on a date. Of course, he wasn't interested in that yet, but that's what made the whole thing more frustrating. He worried that he would never mature enough to ask a girl out and give her the attention she deserved and that he would die alone and lonely.

The truth was that many girls had crushes on Matty but he knew that those girls were only attracted to him on a superficial level. If they knew the real Matty with all his insecurities, they would run and hide.

Matty's parents finally realized something was wrong with their son on the family's annual week-long trip to the shore. It was a time of year Matty usually looked forward to, but not this season.

For the first time in his life, Matty felt nervous about leaving his house overnight and being away from the town which was so familiar to him. Plus, he wasn't in the mood for playing pranks with his cousins or listening to his grandparents tell stories of their childhoods. Life just felt too heavy and too dark for all of that.

Matty briefly considered asking his parents for permission to skip the trip and stay home by himself. He would prefer thinking and pining away in the woods in solitude to playing beach ball and getting sunburn. But he quickly discarded the idea. His parents wouldn't understand.

As the family of three drove to the shore with boogie boards and fishing rods in tow, Matty didn't chatter the whole ride down. This was the first sign to his mother that something was not right. Her son had always had so much to say before about plans to learn to surf or stories from trips past. This year he was quiet. He listened to his music through earbuds for almost the entire duration of their journey except for when he slept and dreamt they were driving back home.

His father was surprised when they stopped for food and Matty declined his father's offer to treat him to a large chocolate shake, one of Matty's favorite guilty pleasures. Matty had told his father he wasn't in the mood.

Throughout the vacation, Matty tried to be the chipper, outgoing boy he once was for the sake of his younger cousins, Max and Maverick, twins aged eleven who admired Matty in every way. Most of the family didn't notice anything was different about the teenager because he tried his best to act like there wasn't.

Perhaps they thought he was a little quieter and less silly than the year before. That was to be expected though because he was growing up. But his mother saw and remembered all of the small things that were different about her little boy, like the way his laughter sounded more forced and less free. The way he slept much more than usual. The way his eyes looked glazed over during a card game and the way he had to be constantly reminded when it was his turn to play. And when it seemed Matty didn't even try to win the family sandcastle building competition.

One night, Matty's mom asked him to walk along the beach with her to watch the sunrise, just the two of them. She wanted to be alone with the boy whom she felt like she was losing. Matty agreed. He wasn't excited about getting up early, but he loved his mother, and he didn't want to make her sad.

Matty and his mom set out before any of the others awoke. Matty held a plastic water bottle. His mother had a warm cup of coffee.

They walked slowly across the dunes. Matty's mother looked up at her son who was a few steps ahead of her.

He was taller than her now. She thought back to when he was a baby and she held him in her arms. She longed for a moment to hold him like that again, to have him be little, to have him need her.

Things seemed much simpler in those days. Matty's mother knew how to comfort him when he was crying. She fed him and he smiled. She sang to him and he laughed. All Matty's mother wanted to do was comfort him now.

For a while, they strolled along in silence. Matty felt at ease. He adored no one more than his mother. While being alone was his preference lately, Matty didn't mind her presence. She had a peace about her that made him feel safe.

"I like this," he said with a smile, the first genuine one his mother had seen in a while.

She smiled back and felt her throat grow tight. She was an easy crier, but she wouldn't, not now. Instead, she reached out and pushed his hair out of his eyes. "I like it too, Matty," she said. "I'm glad you came with me."

"Would you have gone without me?" he asked.

His mother laughed. "No, but it is beautiful, isn't it?" she said, gazing out at the soft peach-colored sun that glowed just above the horizon and the water that glistened below.

"It is," Matty whispered. Beautiful wasn't a word he had used to describe the world recently, but he wasn't lying. The sun was beautiful, and so was the reliable sound of waves crashing, the feeling of soft sand under his feet, and the moment alone with his mother.

It was so beautiful; he sat down to take it all in. His mother followed her son's lead. And so they sat with their feet where the tide ended, looking out at the endless sea.

"I love you," his mother said, still wondering how her only baby had grown before her eyes.

"I love you too," Matty replied, keeping his gaze steady ahead of him.

"Matty, is something wrong?" his mother asked quietly with fear that she might offend her son with the question.

Matty shook his head. "No, why would you think that?"

His mother hesitated. "You've seemed a little off, that's all. I don't know. Maybe I'm just imagining something. I only want to make sure you're happy," his mother said while drawing a heart in the sand Matty couldn't see.

Matty nodded. Part of him wanted to spill everything to his mother. He knew he could. But what if it broke her heart? Worse yet, what if it broke his pride?

"Are you happy, Mom?" he asked, trying to get the attention off of himself before he began to cry.

The question threw his mother off guard. Of course, she was, she thought. But her happiness seemed so trivial ever since the day she found out she had conceived Matty. She had wanted to have a baby for so long but couldn't. If only Matty knew the countless prayers he had answered! Simply being a mother brought her a kind of joy that surpassed mere happiness.

"Oh, Matty," she sighed. "You really are the sweetest." Matty blushed at the compliment. His mother continued, "I always have joy because I have you, but as your mom, I can only ever be as happy as you are."

There was quiet for a moment as Matty considered his mother's words. If she could only be as happy as he was, then she really couldn't be that happy at all. Matty knew that his mother deserved to be happy. It wouldn't be right of him to be the one who limited his mother's happiness, he thought.

Matty knew it was time for him to tell her the truth, but he was afraid. Closing himself off from others and bottling up his feelings had become a lonely but comfortable lifestyle. What lay ahead of him would be open, honest, and vulnerable, and it would hurt for a while before things could get better because Matty would no longer be living in a sense of denial.

So, he took a deep breath, dug his toes further into the sand, and prepared himself to tell his mother what the last six months had been like for him because he loved her.

"Mom, I don't know why," Matty stuttered, "but I just don't feel the way I used to. There is no good reason for me to be unhappy, but I am constantly. Everything is too much for me to handle, and I feel like I'm a big screw-up. I can't do anything right. None of my friends understand. Everything is so uncertain. I can't stand it. All I want to do is be alone, but then I'm just so lonely I can hardly bear it."

Matty's mother felt grief. She was glad her son had been honest and she was determined to help him feel better, but it still stung to hear that her baby was hurting. She wondered if there was anything she could have done to prevent Matty from feeling this pain.

"Matty, love, I'm so sorry," his mother cooed, rubbing circles on his back with the palm of her hand. "You know your dad and I love you so much. You're our whole world, Matty. We're going to do whatever it takes to get you feeling better."

Matty nodded and rested his head on his mother's shoulder like he used to do when he was a little boy, and she was reading him bedtime stories. Her words had comforted him, but they didn't take away the sadness or the fear of the future.

"I'm sorry," Matty whispered as his mother petted his wavy, thick hair.

"Don't apologize for your feelings, Matty. It's okay. I'm so glad you told me. I was missing your jokes and your smirks and your singing in the shower, but now we have a chance of getting those things back."

Matty felt a tear roll down his face. He wiped it off quickly, hoping his mother hadn't seen it, but she had.

"You know," she whispered in the kindest, gentlest way a woman ever had, "crying is thought to be weak, but I think those who cry openly are the very bravest of all."

Matty couldn't hold it in anymore. Weeks of pent-up feelings came pouring out as tears on his mother's cotton tee shirt. Matty's mother was proud of him. She knew there is nothing more frightening for a man than to admit he is not okay.

"Thank you, Mom," Matty said, gratefully after he had cried all he could.

"You're welcome, Matty. Try your best to keep your chin up for the rest of the trip if you can. There's only one day left. Then, we can sort everything out with your father when we get back home."

"I can do that," Matty responded dutifully.

"It looks like it's finally morning, now," Matty's mother said because the colors of the sunrise had faded into a light blue sky and a bright yellow sun.

"Yeah," Matty agreed.

"Come on," his mother said, "Let's head back. Your grandfather will be up soon, and he'll like me to get breakfast ready."

With that, the two walked back to their rental. Matty felt like a weight had been lifted from his shoulders, but he knew there was a very long, uphill hike ahead of him.

3 THE TRIPLETS

Laila had been an only child for most of her life. She hadn't minded it either. There were times when she wondered what it would be like to have an older brother to teach her how to swim or a little sister to have tea parties with, but she didn't think of it often because she was content being the center of her parents' attention. She also enjoyed playing whatever she wanted whenever she wanted to play it.

Her grandmother who lived a few houses down from Laila's parents' home affectionately called her, "my little fairy" because of her capricious, mysterious, and independent personality. And of course, because she had a delicate appearance and a slight frame that seemed very fragile even to the old woman.

The little fairy, Laila, was the child of two artists. Her mother was a talented potter with her own public studio. She taught ceramics classes to both children and adults. Laila's father was a photographer who insisted on the use of real film whether he was hired to photograph a wedding, take photos of flowers for a magazine, or was simply capturing a family moment on Christmas morning.

Up until she was twelve and a half, Laila had enjoyed most moments of her childhood. She grew up painting or making trinkets out of clay with her mother, finding the most magnificent birds in the forest to photograph with her father on the weekends, and learning all of her grandmothers' family recipes after school. Life had been simple, lovely, and easy.

Everything changed for Laila though when her mother became pregnant again. When her parents excitedly announced to Laila at the end of her sixth-grade year that she was going to be a big sister, Laila was shocked.

She had assumed her parents were done having children. They had never mentioned the idea of having a second child to Laila before. Laila was excited initially, although she could hardly believe the news. There were so many things she could teach this little one and she knew the baby would be very cute.

Her excitement turned to nervousness though when weeks later an ultrasound revealed her mother was expecting not one baby, but three! Laila was going to be the significantly older sibling to triplets.

Laila's parents were thrilled, or at least that's how they acted in front of their daughter. Laila tried to match their enthusiasm, but on the inside Laila was nervous. What would it be like when the size of the Jennings household doubled? What if she wasn't able to sleep at night because of the sound of three crying newborns? Would she have to learn how to change a diaper? So many questions stirred in Laila's head and she didn't know the answers to any of them.

Gradually, Mrs. Jennings' tummy grew and grew until Laila thought it might just burst at any moment. As the spare bedroom was converted into a nursery and doctor's appointments became more frequent for Laila's mother, Laila focused on her schoolwork and hobbies. She had a sinking feeling that things were going to become very different very soon, so she tried her hardest to enjoy every moment of life as she knew it before her world changed.

Finally, the day arrived for the triplets to be born. Laila stood around awkwardly as her mother and father ran through the checklist of things they would need before leaving for the hospital. Laila was dropped off at her grandmother's house where she would wait until the call came for them to drive up to the hospital and meet Laila's new siblings.

"Grandma?" Laila asked as the two sat across from each other at the kitchen table eating pancakes and bacon.

"Yeah, Laila," her father's mother smiled while her light-blue eyes twinkled.

"I have a question," Laila said hesitantly.

"Well, you know you can ask me anything," Laila's

grandmother encouraged her.

"I know, but it might not be very nice," Laila confided in a completely serious tone. Grandma chuckled and Laila blushed.

"I've seen a lot of not very nice things in my time. I think I'll be able to handle one more from my little fairy," she winked.

"Ok, then," Laila said, taking a deep breath in. "The truth is, I know I'm going to love these triplets, but I'm worried that things are going to change and I'm not going to like it," Laila frowned.

"Aww, my sweet Laila," Grandma said, reaching out to pat the pre-teen's hand. "You're right. You are going to love your brothers and sisters instantly, as soon as you see them. That's the tricky thing about babies. And you're right about your life-changing. It will. Sometimes you'll love it and sometimes, well, you won't love it so much. But you'll never want to change it because those siblings will become a part of you."

Listening to her Grandma's advice made Laila feel assured that everything was going to be okay. Laila hoped that one day she would be able to be as kind and understanding of a grandmother as her Grandma was.

The two passed the rest of their time playing cards and watching the local news channel, but neither of them cared about who won "Go Fish" or what the school board would be voting on next week. All they could think about was Laila's mother and the babies. They hoped that everybody was safe and well. As they anxiously awaited a call from Laila's father, they imagined what the children would look like, what they would be named, and who they would become.

Laila's heart felt like it was about to explode as she heard the sound of Grandma's landline ringing. It was her father relaying the news that their little girl and two little boys were healthy. Mother had had a smooth delivery and was now recovering. Grandma and Laila could now come to meet the babies.

"Grandma, what are their names? Did Dad say what they look like? Are they big?" Laila asked enthusiastically on the ten-minute drive to the hospital.

"I don't know, Laila. He didn't say, but everyone is healthy. That's the most important thing," Grandma said.

Laila voiced her agreement, but she was hardly listening to her grandmother. She couldn't think straight. She hadn't been this ecstatic since her parents surprised her with a trip to Disney World when she was six years old.

"Hey, big sister!" Laila's father greeted her as she arrived in the labor and delivery waiting room, "and Grandma times three," he added, winking at his mother.

"Dad, can we go see them?" Laila asked hurriedly while returning his hug.

"Alright, come on, we can look at them through the nursery window. The firstborn was Aaron, then came Charlotte, and Benjamin."

"Oh, Dad! Those are the best names I've ever heard," Laila exclaimed, squeezing her father's hand. He could already tell that she was going to be a wonderful older sibling.

Laila, her father, and her grandmother stood at the window looking in at the three tiny babies in bassinets. Laila smiled and studied each little nose, ear, eye, and mouth on her sister and brothers.

"Aren't they beautiful?" Grandma whispered into Laila's ear.

Laila was in such awe that all she could murmur was, "Yeah."

After a long gaze in at her siblings and trip up to her mother's room for a visit, Laila and her grandmother returned home for dinner and a movie night in. Laila's grandmother told stories about when Laila was a baby. Laila couldn't wait until she had stories to tell about her siblings.

That night as Laila lay trying to fall asleep on the big king-sized bed in her grandmother's guest room, she thanked God for Aaron, Charlotte, and Benjamin. Before she closed her eyes, she thought to herself that she was the luckiest girl in the world.

In a few days, Laila's mother and the babies were able to come home and that's when the real chaos began.

First, it was difficult for Laila to remember which baby was Aaron and which baby was Benjamin. All the babies looked like swaddles of blankets with the same,scrunched-up faces but Aarron and Benjamin were both boys and dressed in blue which made it more difficult for Laila to tell them apart.

Then, there was the issue of Laila's mother. She was tired, stressed out, and frustrated all the time. Laila understood why and didn't hate her mother for it, but of course, it did worry Laila who felt like no matter how many bottles she fetched or onesies she washed she could never relieve the constant tension her mother lived with.

What Laila disliked the most about the triplets' arrival was the time they took away from the special moments she used to share with her mom and dad. Her parents cared about her and loved her, but that didn't change the fact that there was no longer someone to listen to her long-winded stories about the ducks in the school's courtyard or to help her with algebra homework. If Laila wasn't independent before, she surely was now.

Of course, there were all the smells and noises and stuff that comes with having three babies in the house. Diapers were stored like canned food in a bunker house. Gurgles, crying, and screams replaced the classic rock music her parents played before.

As challenging as the baby days were for everyone in the house, Laila never felt resentment toward Aaron, Charlotte, or Benjamin. Principally, Laila had an intrinsic love for all forms of life, and especially for life as cute as the triplets. Emotionally, Laila already felt so bonded and connected to her siblings that even if they gave her headaches, she still loved them.

Time passed and the Jennings children grew. The triplets learned how to walk on two feet. Laila learned what it felt like to crush on someone who didn't share the same feelings. The triplets survived their first day of preschool and Laila survived her first high school dance. The triplets got their first participation trophies for four-year-old soccer and Laila got her first real job at Gail's Ice Cream Shack.

She was nervous on her first day on the job as most sixteen-year-olds are when they've never worked before. But after a few weeks, she learned the ropes and felt comfortable with making all of the frozen treats on the menu.

Shortly after Laila started, another kid from her high school was hired. His name was Matty.

In Laila's eyes, Matty was everything she wasn't, popular, sports-inclined, and wealthy. In Matty's eyes, Laila was everything he wasn't, carefree, creative, and self-important.

Both Laila and Matty's perceptions of each other were not entirely accurate. Laila did have a healthy amount of self-love, but she didn't always feel validated and she had her share of insecurities. Matty was admired by his peers, but that didn't mean he had many sincere friends.

Laila and Matty were awkward on their first shift together, but as time passed and they were forced to spend time together they became an unusual set of friends. Polite small-talk grew into Matty becoming an interested and dedicated listener to stories and weekly updates on the Jenning triplets' antics. Laila learned that Matty told really funny jokes.

But when Gail's Ice Cream Shack closed up for the season and Matty and Laila went back to school, the two drifted apart. Matty went back to the cool table where he felt very lonely and Laila went back to eating at whatever table of geeky kids would accept her in as a guest that day.

Sometimes though, Matty would glance over at Laila and wonder what was going on in the mind of hers that he knew was a fascinating place. And sometimes Laila looked over at Matty and wondered how such a beautiful boy could have a smile on his face and the saddest eyes she had ever seen at the same time.

4 EXPERIMENTAL STUDY

When Matty's family returned from their beach vacation, they sat down together and discussed how Matty was feeling. Matty felt more uncomfortable spilling to his father than he had to just his mother alone.

In his fifteen years of life, he couldn't remember a time he had seen his father cry, and now Matty was sitting across from him and bawling for reasons he couldn't understand.

"But why do you feel this way?" his father would ask after Matty explained that he was tortured with panic attacks triggered by the oddest things like a rapping on his window at night, an old picture of himself with a bad haircut, or a sad story he saw in the news.

His feelings weren't rational, and he knew that, but understanding that his feelings were illogical did not change the fact that his feelings were controlling and almost destroying every aspect of his life.

"I don't know why," Matty sniffled with his head in his hands.

"It's okay, Matty," his mother interjected, "sometimes we don't understand and all we can do is try to make it better."

Matty's father nodded reluctantly to show that he agreed with his wife. This was all new and unexpected to him. It didn't make sense to him why Matty was depressed. Matty's father remembered feeling on top of the world during his high school years, and he didn't see any reason why his son shouldn't be as well.

However, Matty's father trusted his wife when she told him that something was wrong with their son and that Matty needed their love and support more than anything else right now. Mental health was not an area of expertise for Mr. Holt, but he would try to be the best dad he could be in this situation for the family he deeply loved.

The family agreed that Matty should seek professional help as his thoughts and feelings were interfering with the quality of his daily life. Moreover, Matty had even lost a few pounds over the summer because his anxiety was causing a loss of appetite.

The first doctor's appointments were rough because it meant explaining to someone outside of his family that he was sad, worried, and had major self-esteem issues. Matty was diagnosed with generalized depression and anxiety.

Matty started attending therapy counseling sessions and began taking a pill every day to help with chemical imbalances contributing to his poor mental and emotional health.

As Matty entered his sophomore year of high school, he was feeling more secure in himself and happier than he had been. He had nerves about the difficult coursework he would be taking and trying out for the varsity soccer team, but his nerves weren't unmanageable or abnormal. Sometimes he would sink back into negative thought patterns, but he fought to keep his mind free of thoughts that made him feel unnecessarily worried, sad, or anxious.

Matty learned ways to deal with his feelings that were positive and effective. His favorite was walking into the forest that lay behind his house and hiking up the mountain until he reached the lookout point and he could see the whole town below him. Everything seemed so small from up there, but Matty felt so big.

Although negative feelings and thoughts never completely disappeared from Matty's life, he was able to enjoy his day to day and function in school. He even got a summer job and although it was boring and tedious at times, Matty didn't mind it because he got to meet a rather curious girl named Laila.

While Matty did everything he could to hide his mental struggles from people outside of his family, he had the strange compulsion to open up to Laila. There was something about her, maybe it was her deep blue eyes or her warm laugh, he didn't know, but he had the desire to share his story with her. Unlike his other friends, Matty felt like Laila would understand.

Matty never mentioned anything to Laila though. Partially because it never came up in conversation and partially because Matty still wasn't ready yet.

Things were well in Matty's life for a couple of years. He started for the varsity soccer team, kept his 4.0 GPA, and was voted prom prince. Matty worked hard for all of those things. Work was a good distraction from the thoughts in his head he didn't want to think about.

Matty's life was fine until suddenly during the fall of his senior year it just wasn't anymore. With so much change coming around the corner of his life and the stress of college and scholarship applications, the panic attacks, the feelings of helplessness, and the self-deprecating thought patterns returned.

Matty had some new feelings too. Like maybe things would be better if he had never been born. He had strange and confusing desires too. Sometimes Matty fantasized about cutting or burning himself. It scared him, and when he tearfully confessed it to his mother, it scared her even more so than it had Matty.

Matty and his family went back to the doctors, psychiatrists, and therapists who had helped him before.

They tried different medications, more therapy, and new relaxation techniques. None of it worked. Matty just felt worse and worse. Somedays he couldn't even get out of bed because the weight of Matty's fears, doubts, and uncertainties kept him down.

Matty's parents were worried. Almost three months had passed and Matty's condition had only worsened despite everything they had done to try to help their son. Matty's father was not typically a religious man, but even he resorted to prayer as a possible cure.

Finally, hope came. There was a clinical study looking for teenage patients with severe depression, that did not improve through traditional treatment methods, to participate in an experimental drug therapy.

The medication had already passed through safety testing; the doctors assured Matty's parents. There was a good chance that Matty might be helped but virtually no chance Matty would be harmed as long as he took the medication as directed.

After discussing the matter and sleeping on it, Matty and his family eagerly accepted the offer to participate in the study. Matty would begin taking an effugium pill at night that winter. He'd be observed and write a log of how he was feeling each day.

If at the end of six months, Matty had experienced improvement and hadn't had major side effects, they would consider allowing Matty to be treated with effugium long-term.

"I'm glad you've decided to try this, Matty," Dr. Hill had said, "I think it could really be life-changing for you."

Matty was skeptical. Life-changing seemed like too extreme of a word to choose, but later he would discover there was no better word to describe how the medication would affect him

5 THE SPRING

Matty took an effugium pill for the first time on a cold night in January. He hadn't expected anything to happen. It usually took weeks for mood stabilizers or antidepressants to take effect. He was shocked and confused when minutes after taking the medication he found himself standing beside a spring in the forest.

The sun was high in the sky and the air was hot. Unlike in a dream, Matty could feel those things, the sensation of the cool water on his skin and the blinding of his eyes by the sun.

Matty had sat by the spring so many times, so many summers that he felt like he was having déjà vu, yet at the same time, the moment was unique and individual. Matty wasn't simply recalling a memory.

Matty removed his sneakers and pulled his shirt off. He eased himself into the shallow spring. The water was only about three feet deep and ten feet wide at its longest point. Matty reclined resting his arms on the soft moss and grass that surrounded the spring.

Matty watched as water bubbled up from a point in the back of the pool of water surrounded by small, smooth stones. Matty looked up at the tall pine trees. He wondered how old each one was. Then he looked down at the bottom of the spring. Matty watched how the water flowed out of the pool into a stream that trickled down the mountain until it reached the flatland, snaked through the town, and eventually joined the larger creek in the park.

Matty felt tranquil and content as he sat in what he considered to be paradise. After a while, he examined his hands and noticed that his fingertips were getting pruney. Matty knew then that he wasn't dreaming as he typically did. His dreams never had details like that.

The moment was almost perfect, Matty thought, but he wished he had someone to share it with. A moment so beautiful deserved to be enjoyed by someone else besides just Matty. But who would ever appreciate just sitting and taking in the surroundings? Surely not Jake or Finn.

To Matty, it seemed like everyone preferred to be doing while he preferred just being. Then, he remembered someone, Laila Jennings. Laila would appreciate just being, he guessed.

He laughed to himself and his laughter echoed on the quiet, still mountain. He was remembering how confidently Laila had read her poem in front of their economics class a few weeks before. Then, he remembered how she had made him a special, hodge-podge milkshake when he was feeling down one summer day.

She had mixed up a bit of every flavor of ice cream and every candy in the store and presented it to Matty with a quirky giggle and a mischievous look in her eyes.

"I made it just for you, Matty," she laughed while urging him to try at least one sip of the thick, green shake.

"Laila, that is possibly the most revolting color a milkshake could ever be. Are you trying to poison me?" Matty teased.

After bantering back and forth for some time, Laila persuaded Matty to take a sip. It was sickeningly sweet, but it wasn't poisonous. Matty wished he could get to know Laila better. She was so different yet not weird at all.

Laila and Matty had gone to school together for the past twelve and a half years. They could have been friends, but they never were. They had never been in the same clique. Matty knew that if his friends saw him hanging out with Laila that they would think it was odd, but now for some reason, Matty thought that he shouldn't care what they thought.

Matty wanted to go back and tell Laila that she was a pretty special person. He wanted to tell her that he liked her poem. He wanted to ask her what her plans were for after graduation.

Suddenly, Matty was back in his bedroom, curled up under his comforter in a pair of sweatpants and an old hoodie. His digital clock read 02:00 a.m.

Matty tried to make sense of what had happened. He had seen, heard, and felt the forest. He had been in the forest. Yet he didn't walk up to the spring. He had just sort of showed up there. Matty couldn't figure out how. He hadn't walked home either. He had just blinked, and the forest turned into his dark bedroom; the cool water transformed into warm sheets.

It certainly wasn't a dream. It was much too real to be that.

Matty thought about it. If he hadn't traveled to the spring or traveled back from the spring and he had returned without any physical changes, like wet hair or a bug bite then, his body hadn't gone anywhere. The experience was all in his mind.

It wasn't a fantasy either because Matty did not have complete control. Matty needed a name to call the experience in his mind, for he knew he would think of it often. First, he thought of "magic trip" but that reminded him too much of *The Magic School Bus*. Plus, it wasn't magic either. It was medicine.

Matty then considered calling it a "hallucination", but it wasn't that. He needed something else. An "escape", that's what he would call it. It was like escaping from reality, escaping from your real body to someplace better. But only for a short time.

Matty closed his eyes and drifted off to sleep feeling very special to have experienced an escape.

6 MEETING ON THE MOUNTAIN

The morning after his first escape, Matty felt refreshed. Somehow he didn't feel as blue. The escape had given him perspective and a good rush of endorphins that made the world seem a little brighter.

After school, Matty decided that even though it was cold and windy he would take a walk on the forest trail behind his home. He needed some time to think about what had happened to him.

The experience wasn't bad at all, Matty thought. In fact, he enjoyed it. However, Matty didn't understand what had happened to him. It was like a dream because he had woken up in his bed yet it wasn't like a dream at all. After all, he was in control of what he touched and what he did and he could see and feel things as if it were real life.

Matty wanted to tell someone about the escape, but he knew that even his mother wouldn't understand. If someone had told Matty about a pill that transports people to other times and places while they sleep, Matty would have thought they were crazy. How could he expect anyone to listen to him and believe his story?

Matty knew that an out-of-body type of experience was not what was supposed to happen on the medication. His mood was supposed to improve, he would feel more calm, likely suffer from fewer panic attacks, and feel less irritable. He was not, however, supposed to fall into wonderland, for lack of a better word.

Matty thought that it would be a good idea to tell his doctors. Even if they did think he was insane at least they would know that the medication had a quite unbelievable side effect. But there was no need for that yet. He would have to experience the pill a few more times to understand what was truly happening.

As Matty had almost reached the end of the trail, he was surprised to see a girl about twenty feet ahead of him. He wondered who else would be crazy enough to be out on a wooded mountain in almost freezing temperatures. It was dangerous. There was a solid inch of snow covering the ground and likely ice in spots too. It was especially unsafe to hike alone. If you got injured, no one would be there to help you.

Matty decided maybe he should be a gentleman and walk the rest of the way down the trail with the girl. He would feel bad if anything happened to her.

"Hello," he said as he approached the girl in a soft voice. She seemed a bit preoccupied so he was careful not to startle her.

The girl turned around quickly and smiled when she saw Matty in front of her. Matty recognized her. It was Laila Jennings and she had a camera.

"Oh, hi, Matty!" Laila said, "What are you doing all the way up here?"

"I was just about to ask you the same question," Matty replied with a grin.

"I'm just practicing my photography," Laila explained gesturing to the camera in her hands. "Everything is so much more beautiful with a coating of snow, isn't it?"

Matty wasn't sure he agreed but knew it would be impolite to say so. "Yeah," he said, "but I'm not a big fan of the cold."

Laila laughed. "Haven't you ever heard: There's no such thing as bad weather, only bad choice of clothes?"

"Yes, but I'm not sure I believe it."

"Oh, I do. Here look," Laila said, pulling up some pictures of the wintry forest on the mountain. The photos were stunning. There was a close-up of a fawn and doe eating berries from a bush, a shot of rabbit tracks in the snow, and a bird's eye view picture of Richardsville that Laila must have gotten from the lookout point.

"Wow," Matty exclaimed, "You really do have a talent."

Laila blushed, "I don't know, but thanks for saying that."

"No, you do. I wouldn't lie to you, Laila," Matty promised surprising Laila with his sudden sincerity.

"Thanks. So, what are you doing up here? It's cold," Laila

said, wrapping her arms around her body.

"Oh yeah, I know. I just needed a place to think. That's all," Matty explained awkwardly. "I'm about to head back down. Come with me before it gets dark."

"Alright," Laila agreed as she began to follow Matty down the trail. "What did you have to think about?" she asked suddenly.

Matty thought Laila's forwardness was a little intrusive. For a split second, he considered telling the truth, but then came up with something better. "Just school and college stuff, that's all."

"Are you excited about next year?" Laila asked. She was.

"Do you want the truth?" Matty replied somewhat snarkily.

"You're supposed to say yes, you know," Laila pointed out.

"Then, yes."

"But it's a no, isn't it?" Laila asked, surprised.

Everyone it seemed was excited to get out of Richardsville. Laila was and Matty had such a good future ahead of him. Out of all the members of their class he should have been the most excited to leave, Laila thought.

"It's a no. Sort of... I don't know," Matty mumbled.

"Why?"

"I really don't know. The future is just kind of, it's just so uncertain. I don't like not knowing things," Matty admitted.

"I think that's what they call an adventure. You know when you don't know what lies around the corner, but you think it might be fun."

"You sure have an interesting way of looking at things."

"I get that a lot," Laila chuckled.

"Hey, that reminds me. I've been wanting to tell you that I thought your poem was nice."

"Oh, the one Ms. Fredericks made me read? That was so humiliating. I thought I was going to die," Laila sighed.

"Who cares about her? She's such a grouch."

"Yeah, I guess so."

"So, what do you really think about Richardsville, then?" Matty implored.

"Well, it's my home. I could never really dislike my home," Laila answered.

"Do you ever get tired of the triplets?" Matty asked remembering all of the stories Laila had shared with him over the last two summers.

Laila laughed. "Well, I'd be lying if I said no. That's the real reason I'm out here. I needed a break. I had to get out of the house. Lottie wouldn't stop pestering me to paint her nails and I didn't want to and the boys were playing their drum kit which makes it impossible for me to think straight. But they're my home too and like I said, I could never really dislike my home."

"That's a clever answer," Matty complimented Laila after warning her to watch out for a slippery rock on the path.

"Now that I've told you what I think, it's only fair that you do the same."

Matty thought for a moment. He'd never lived anywhere else besides Richardsville neither had Laila for that matter. He hadn't spent much time thinking about whether he liked it or not because when you're growing up you don't have a real say in where you live, so there's no point in worrying about it. "It's alright. I've never really thought about it. Maybe I would feel this way no matter where I lived, but do you ever feel like you just want to get away like you just want to kind of escape for a moment- and then come back? You know what I mean?"

"I do. I have lots of places I escape to when things get to be a little too much. I come up here to wander around, I go to the park sometimes, and then, of course, there's my bedroom which is kind of like my little hideout. My Grandma lives down the street from me so when things get unbearable, I go and visit her. She makes everything better," Laila told Matty.

"Yeah, yeah. That's kind of what I'm talking about." Matty was excited because Laila's answer made him hopeful that someday he would be able to share his secret with her.

"Do you think that you'll work at Gail's again next summer?" Laila asked.

"Probably," Matty supposed.

"It's nice to have money," Laila professed.

"That's true."

Now, Laila and Matty had almost reached the end of the forest trail at the bottom of the mountain. Matty had something he had been wanting to say to Laila, but he was feeling nervous about it.

"Hey, Laila…" he started just as she was about to open her

car door and he was about to wander back into his backyard.

"What's up?"

"I know that we don't know each other that well and we aren't really friends in school, but I was wondering, if maybe, I mean if you want to, we could hang out sometime," Matty stuttered.

Laila was flattered. People didn't ask her to hang out outside of school very often, so this was a special moment. "Yeah, I would like that," she said enthusiastically.

"Great! I'll just text you some time and we can talk again. You have a lot of interesting things to say."

Laila smiled as she unlocked the door to her old used Chevy, "You too. You're more interesting than they give you credit for, Matty."

"Thanks. I mean, I guess," Matty said.

"Goodbye, Matty," Laila waved as she slid into her car.

"Goodbye," he waved and watched as the girl drove away.

Matty walked back into his house with a newfound optimism.

"How was your walk, honey?" his mother asked, handing him a cup of tea just the way he liked it as Matty struggled to warm up from the cold.

"It was good," Matty said and this time his mother could tell that he meant it.

"I'm glad to hear that."

"And you know what, Mom?" Matty added.

"What, Matty?"

"I think this new medication is going to make it okay."

Matty's mother found her son's words bittersweet. No parent wants their child's wellbeing to be dependent on medication, but every parent wants their child to be okay, first. Mrs. Holt kissed her son gently on the forehead and petted his rosy cheeks which were still freezing from the wind.

"I hope so, Matty, but even if they don't I know you'll be my strong boy and make it through until everything is alright again. I know you can. I really do," she said.

"I know," Matty assured her. Then, he wrapped his arms around his mother and everything was okay for a moment.

7 INDEPENDENCE DAY

Every night for the next three days, Matty took his effugium. And every night for the next three days, he experienced an escape, but they weren't all like the first.

On the second night, Matty escaped to Christmastime when he was a child. It was strange because he could think like an adult, but his parents spoke to him like he was five years old, which made sense because he was, of course, in a five-year-old's body. It was fun to open up the presents and eat chocolate chip cookies and feel safe. But eventually, he started thinking about the Christmas presents he had received as a seventeen-year-old and how much he wanted to play the guitar his uncle had gotten for him. It was then that he found himself back in his bed again just like the night before.

On the third night, Matty escaped to a strange place and time he hadn't been before. He was in his teenage body but dressed in 1950s' style clothing and watching a drive-in movie. There was popcorn and music playing, and everything seemed upbeat, but then Matty realized that he was just watching people he didn't know have a good time. He started to wish that he had some of his friends with him to watch the movie, and that's when he woke up in his room.

On the fourth night, Matty escaped to an entirely new time. He was older, almost fifty he figured, and was sailing along a slow river in a motorboat. It was nice, but lonely too, and Matty didn't like the way his 'old' body felt. It was wrinkly, and his hands hurt whenever he tried to use them to fish or to open a can of soda. Matty started to think about his strong, fast, handsome younger body. He longed to be back in it again. Then, like magic, he was lying in the exact position he had been seconds after he had taken the effugium pill.

Matty wrote in his log every day how he was feeling on the pills. The first day, he said much the same, so as not to create suspicion, and because he was very unsure of what had happened to him. On the second day, he wrote that his mood felt improved and he was feeling more energized. On the third day, he wrote that he hadn't experienced any panic attacks or episodes of crippling anxiety for over seventy-two hours. On the fourth day, he wrote that he thought he was feeling more grounded.

What Matty wrote was partially true, at least some of it, but also a bit of a bluff. Matty was enjoying his escapes very much, but he didn't know how to explain it to anyone, so he kept it to himself. He was worried if he told his parents or his doctors they would take him off the medication, and he didn't want that.

Matty's mood did improve with the effugium. It wasn't that it washed away all of the worries or that it made him feel high, or that it increased the feel-good chemicals. It might have been doing some of those things; Matty didn't know. What he was sure of though was that it was distracting him from all of the present realities he didn't want to deal with. Even when he wasn't in an escape, he was thinking about them all the time. They gave him something to look forward to at the end of the day. Because Matty spent more time going to good places in his mind, he felt better.

He didn't know if it was good or bad to be detached from reality, but he didn't care either. Matty was becoming obsessed with the idea of escaping and the memories of it. In some sort of way, it was addictive.

Matty wanted to tell someone about his escapes. He felt like if he didn't, he would explode. Somehow Matty felt like the best person to tell would be Laila Jennings, but he couldn't just tell her about it. Matty wanted her to experience an escape as well. He knew that would be the only way she could truly understand it.

A genius idea popped into Matty's head. His parents were going to a wedding next weekend. Matty would have the house to himself for forty-eight hours. That would be the perfect time to invite Laila over. He hoped she would say yes. It would be such a blow to Matty if Laila refused.

Matty was especially glad to have the escapes to think about on this particular week because he had just suffered from one of the most traumatic school experiences in his life. Matty had been caught cheating on his end-of-the-semester Calculus final.

Matty hadn't meant to cheat. He really hadn't. He was just so tired the day of the exam and because partner work was usually encouraged in class, Matty instinctually leaned forward to see Finn's paper. When the teacher confronted Matty about it, he didn't buy into Matty's honest claim that it was an unintentional accident, and that he hadn't even copied off Finn because he remembered that it was an exam and not just a classroom activity.

Cheating was a big deal at Richardsville High as it is at most schools. Matty should have been given a zero on the exam according to school policy, but because he was a favorite the teacher gave him a second chance to complete the midterm before school the next day. Unfortunately, though, the teacher was not able to do anything to get Matty out of the standard three days of detention.

Of course, the whole ordeal was very upsetting to Matty. He had had a perfect school record until this point, and it was all ruined because of something he didn't even mean to do. Matty worried that it would affect his admissions offers to universities and his good reputation amongst the Richardsville staff. He worried about what his peers would think and say about him. And worst of all, he had to deal with his parents' disappointment.

His parents were, thankfully, more gracious than Matty had expected. Grades and school were always important to them and they made sure that Matty knew that, but they realized everyone breaks a rule or messes up from time to time so, they took it easy on their emotionally fragile son. Matty's parents punished him by grounding him from his car, but only for a few days.

As horrible as the cheating scandal seemed to Matty at the time, it did allow him to see Laila again. Laila liked to stay late at school to work on her art projects, and coincidentally the art room was where detention was being held on that Friday afternoon.

Laila didn't pay much attention to Matty, and neither did the art teacher. They were both busy working on their own things and, so Matty just sat in the front of the classroom and did his homework quietly. Maybe detention wasn't so bad, Matty thought.

Laila finished her painting ten minutes before Matty's detention was officially over, but she didn't want to leave without him.

"Ms. Wells," she said quietly to the teacher who she considered more of a friend, "I'm giving Matty a ride home and, well, since I'm finished with my work I was wondering if you could let him off the hook a little early and we can all get out of here."

The young Ms. Wells smiled. "Sure, Laila," she said under her breath. "Matty, kiddo," she called out, "You can go home."

Matty looked up bashfully and slid his belongings into his bag and then his bag over his shoulder, "Thanks," he said as he walked toward the door with Laila standing a few yards behind him, "Have a nice day, Ms. Wells," he added.

"Thanks, Matty. You as well and you too, Laila," Ms. Wells said as she began to wash the pile of dirty paintbrushes other students had left behind.

"Hey," Laila shouted to Matty, who had gotten ahead of her in the hallway.

He turned around and waved but did not smile.

"What's wrong?" Laila asked, slightly offended as she caught up with him.

"Oh, nothing," Matty said, "You didn't have to do that. That's all."

Laila blushed. "Oh, you overheard that?"

"Yeah, so thanks, I guess."

"Sure. No problem. Why'd ya get detention anyway?" Laila asked when, in fact, she did know. Everyone did. News travels fast in a small school. Especially when it's about the hometown hero who fell.

Matty blushed and rolled his eyes, "As if you don't know," he said as kindly as he could. He knew his response wasn't very polite, but neither was her question.

"What? I don't," Laila lied. She had to deny that she knew because she didn't want Matty to think she was rude for asking him to admit his mistake to her.

Matty then remembered that he wanted someone to share his escapes with, so he decided to play a game. "Would you like to know?"

Laila was a little caught off guard by the way Matty was acting. "Not really," Laila replied as they stepped into the cold afternoon.

"Well, would you like to hang out, then?" Matty asked, changing the subject.

Laila studied Matty's face for a moment. What was up with this boy? He was just being cold, and now he wanted to hang out.

"I mean, I guess so. If you want to," Laila mumbled.

"Actually, I have something I really want to show you back at my house," Matty said.

"Are you sure your parents won't mind me stopping by?"

"No."

"Really?"

"Yeah, they won't mind because they won't know because they're out of town," Matty smirked.

"Okay, then. You could have just said so." Laila felt relieved because meeting new adults always made her feel a little uncomfortable.

Matty shrugged. "Do you mind driving?" he asked sheepishly. "I'm grounded."

"Yeah, no problem," Laila answered.

Laila felt a little embarrassed having Matty in her car because it was much older and dirtier than the car Matty drove to school. Plus, the passenger's and back seats were filled with empty coffee cups, extra sweatshirts, random pieces of paper, and books belonging to the triplets.

"Sorry about everything," Laila said, gesturing to the car as Matty got in.

"No, it's okay. I'm just glad not to have to walk home," Matty admitted.

Laila turned the radio on as they started to drive to make things less awkward. Of course, Laila was used to listening to a

Beatles/U2 mixed CD in the car, but she thought Matty wouldn't like it, so she resorted to a pop station instead.

Shake It Off by Taylor Swift came blasting through the speakers right away. Laila was surprised and delighted when Matty started singing along. He knew all of the words, and it made Laila laugh out of pure joy. Who would have guessed that Matty would be into Taylor Swift? Surely not his friends on the soccer team, Laila thought.

"You've memorized it?" Laila giggled.

"Yeah, why haven't you?" Matty countered. "It's only like three words."

"I'm not really into the pop scene."

"Oh, come on. Don't be like that. I bet you're one of those girls who only listens to indie music just to be quirky," Matty kidded.

"I'm not!"

"You know what I think, Laila?"

"What?"

"I think that people should listen to music that makes them happy because otherwise what's the point?" Matty said, very seriously.

"Well, I think you're right, then- for the first time today," Laila agreed.

Matty chuckled sardonically, then gave Laila directions to his house. They drove the rest of the way to Matty's house in silence until he said, "I'm a narc."

"What?" Laila exclaimed.

"You asked me why I had detention, and I told you."

"Liar," Laila replied, braking quickly because she almost missed a stop sign, "You cheated, and I actually think it's a little funny."

"Why?" Matty asked, genuinely as they drove down the street that led to his home.

"Because you're supposed to be Mr. Perfect, and now everyone knows that you're not."

"No," Matty said, shaking his head.

"What do you mean, no?" Laila asked as she parked outside of his large, white suburban residence.

"I mean, I was never supposed to Mr. Perfect. That's all in their heads. I've always known I'm not," Matty answered, looking Laila straight in the eyes. Laila wondered if anyone had ever been as honest with her as Matty had at that moment. She didn't think they had.

Laila bit her lip like she always did when she was nervous, "I'm not perfect, but everyone knows it," Laila exhaled.

"And that's the way it should be," Matty replied. Laila wasn't sure what Matty meant by that, so she decided to change the topic.

"So, are we going to hang out or what?"

"Oh yeah, let's go," Matty said, swinging the car door open. "I'm really glad you agreed to come over, by the way. I've been wanting to get to know you better for a while," he explained as Laila locked the car doors.

"There's not much to know about me. But you, it almost seems like you're a completely different person when I talk to you alone than when I see you in school," Laila said as they walked up the driveway.

"I can't really figure that one out myself. I guess I'm still trying to learn who I am. I don't know which one of me is the real me. Sorry if that sounds a little crazy," Matty rambled before opening the door to his parent's grand house. Or at least it was in grand in Laila's eyes.

"No, I don't- I don't think it's crazy at all," Laila countered as she entered Matty's immaculate house. She admired the chandeliers hanging from the ceiling in the entryway and the dining room. Laila stood awkwardly looking at the paintings the family had hung on the wall and the gorgeous floor to ceiling windows that illuminated the living room.

The girl, still in her winter coat, looked over at Matty and saw he was climbing the steps, "Come on," he said, "I told you, my parents are away. Follow me, make yourself at home."

"But where are you going?" Laila asked.

"Upstairs," he said, stating the obvious.

Laila thought briefly about protesting, but then she just decided to follow him. She was curious to find out what the inside of a rich family's house looked like.

As Laila's eyes examined the second floor, she noticed a grandfather clock and some old, framed black and white photos. There was a family tree painted on the hallway, and there were no legos or Barbie dolls scattered on the floor. It was almost the opposite of Laila's home.

Laila wasn't paying attention to where Matty was leading her and sooner than later, she found herself sitting on his bed, looking out the window at the view of the mountain from the backside of his house. It was stunningly beautiful, and Laila felt jealous that Matty got to wake up to it every morning.

After a few seconds, it hit Laila that she had done something wrong. Her parents told her a million times, under no circumstances, to go into a boy's bedroom especially alone and especially when his parents weren't home. Laila thought she should leave, but she didn't want to.

"I shouldn't be in your bedroom," Laila said and started to walk toward the door.

"Probably not," Matty said kicking his shoes off into the closet, "but I'm not attracted to you, so really I might as well just be one of your girlfriends."

Laila found his comment hurtful. She felt like she shouldn't have cared, but she did. Of course, she couldn't let on that he had hurt her so she said, "Fine, then. I'm only attracted to men who aren't miserable, so we're all good. I guess."

Matty smiled. "Touché," he said, giving Laila an approving pat on the shoulder.

Laila sat down on the bed and watched as Matty reached into his side drawer and took out two little white pills.

"Here," Matty said, handing one to Laila.

"Matty, what is this? I can't just take random drugs from you," Laila exclaimed, surprised at his behavior.

"Shh…" Matty said lying down on the bed to face the ceiling. "It's just an antidepressant. Trust me. It's completely safe. Doctors prescribe stuff like this to people all the time. You might be able to be on them if you wanted to be on them. Maybe you should be. I've noticed you've seemed a little melancholy these past couple of years," he said, flickering his eyes closed.

"Please trust me. You're not going to get high or do anything stupid off of this. It's going to make things feel better. It's how I get through life and I want to share it with you because I think you deserve to experience a good, happy life, Laila Holt," Matty added, hoping to convince her.

Laila had a choice to make. Was she going to trust this boy or was she going to make the decision that would make her parents proud? A thousand thoughts and scenarios flashed through her mind as she examined the white, circular pill in the center of her hand.

Laila started to think that maybe Matty was right. The last couple of years had been tough. High school is harder than people assume. Laila tried to look on the bright side of everything, but sometimes life was just sad and stressful and boring and heavy.

So, Laila took a deep breath and told herself it was okay to make one foolish decision as a teenager. She glanced over at Matty who was lying peacefully on his back. He had said that the pills were antidepressants and that they were prescribed by a doctor. Laila figured whatever medication it was, it couldn't be that bad.

Against all of her better judgment, Laila closed her eyes and popped the pill into her mouth. She lay down next to Matty and took a deep breath in. Then, all of a sudden, Laila opened her eyes and she didn't see Matty's ceiling anymore.

Laila looked around, startled because everything around her felt so familiar, yet so different at the same time. She was sitting in the grass at the town park. Laila noticed her hands were smaller and her legs were shorter.

She wondered what happened to her. Was she high? Had she died?

Laila checked out her surroundings. The sky was blue, the kind of blue that makes you feel lucky to live in such a beautiful world. The sun was high in the sky, and it felt warm on Laila's bare legs and shoulders. Children were playing tag on a playground a few yards away from where Laila was situated under a tree.

Laila was wearing a red tank top and athletic shorts. She reached up and touched her hair. It was in pigtails. She slipped off her light-up sneakers and looked at her foot. Laila noticed the heart-shaped birthmark on the inside of her big toe that she'd always had.

She realized that she was herself, but her younger self. Laila wasn't sure exactly how old she was, but she figured somewhere between seven and nine.

The thing that was hardest for Laila to comprehend was that even though she was in a child's body, she didn't have a child's mind. She was herself, with all of her memories, just in a different time, body, and place.

Laila assumed she must have been on an acid trip when a little boy with glistening brown eyes and curls peeking out of his Phillies baseball cap came running up to her.

It was Matty, but a younger Matty.

"Hi, Laila," he squeaked out in a voice Laila hadn't heard in years. "You look scared," he said and reached down to grab her hand and pull her up so that she was standing next to him under a big oak tree.

"Where are we?" Laila asked, shaking as she stood next to him still trying to process what had happened.

"We're in the park," Matty said matter-of-factly. "It's the Fourth of July. 2009, I believe," he explained, pointing to his mother who was wearing a t-shirt with an American flag printed on the front and the year 2009 in a large-sized font.

"This is a dream?" Laila questioned, staring at Matty suspiciously.

Matty hesitated for a second, then shook his head. "No, it's real. I don't know. We can feel everything and everyone else is really experiencing today as they would have nine years ago. The only difference is that we get to experience it with adult minds and relive everything however we want to again."

Laila still couldn't believe what was happening. "I want to go back," she stuttered. She was terrified.

"No, no. It's okay. Come on. Let's go catch some minnows in the lake," Matty waved as he began skipping over to the shallow creek not far away.

As scared as Laila was, she followed him. Laila thought that maybe he had been there before. She would need him to be her guide.

As Laila ran behind him toward the creek, she saw faces she remembered. Less-aged versions of her mother and father were cooking hot dogs and hamburgers on a charcoal grill. The boys and girls from Laila's elementary Sunday school class were chasing each other around the playground.

Then, Laila remembered what day it was. It was the day of the annual Independence Day picnic hosted by 1st Methodist Church. Laila's family hadn't gone in years, not since the triplets were born, but she remembered it well.

Warm, fuzzy memories rushed through Laila's head as she remembered all of the festivities she used to look forward to on this day every year, water balloon fights, rainbow-colored snow cones, family softball, and of course sitting on her dad's shoulders to watch the fireworks display at the end of the night.

Laila's memories were interrupted when she reached the creek. Matty was already in up to his ankles. When Laila was younger, she used to be afraid of creatures hiding around rocks and would barely venture into the creek where the other children loved to play. However, she was older now and she wasn't afraid anymore so she slipped her shoes and socks off her tiny feet and jumped into the cool, rushing water.

She closed her eyes for a second as the mossy stones tickled her feet, the breeze ran through her tied-up hair, and the water sprayed tiny droplets up onto her face.

Briefly, Laila thought about how that moment would have made the perfect subject for a transcendentalist poem and then she laughed out loud because she realized how silly it was for a nine-year-old to consider the works of Emerson or Thoreau.

Of course, Laila wasn't really a nine-year-old that's just what she appeared to be and what everyone took her as except for Matty who knew the truth.

"We're actually here," Laila whispered to Matty as he grabbed her hand and led her further into the creek.

"I know. Isn't it amazing? Aren't you glad you decided to try it?" Matty asked in a high voice that made Laila want to giggle.

"Yes," she answered honestly while reaching down to capture a minnow in her hand, "I don't fully understand what's going on, but I think I like it."

In one swift motion, Matty reached down and caught a minnow in his hands.

"Look," he said, showing Laila his cupped hand with water trickling out of it and an inch-long fish frantically wiggling while his body gleamed in the midday sun.

"Good job, Matty," Laila said, patting him on the back.

It was weird for Laila to pal around with Matty as a child because during their elementary and middle school years they weren't very close friends at all. Laila kept to herself and played with the other shy girls. Matty was usually the center of attention, kicking a soccer ball around with his friends or playing the class clown.

"We didn't hang out together on this day, did we?" Laila asked knowing it was unlikely.

Matty shook his head while taking a few steps further into the water. "I doubt it. I think I would have been over there," he said pointing to a group of boys on paddle boats in the pond.

"So, what's going on, exactly?" Laila wondered.

"Well, I don't know exactly. It's not really something that can be easily understood and I don't really know how it's happening, but from what I've gathered over the past week of taking these, these antidepressants is that they let you experience the past, or the future, or other alternate realities without changing history."

"What you're saying, then, is that we didn't time travel, right?"

"I wouldn't say so. It's more like we're dreaming, but together and we can really smell, touch, hear, and feel things. It's not really like lucid dreaming because I never know where I'm going to go when I pop one of those pills into my mouth, and I can't control the surroundings or the people who are there. All we get to really do is escape real life for a moment and enjoy another time in history," Matty explained.

At that point, Laila was starting to understand what was going on, as well as she could at least. It was all so strange, but it was also new and exciting. Laila didn't want to leave. She felt curious and happy. What Matty said was true. For once in a very long time, Laila didn't have any sadness, none at all.

Laila looked over to the oak tree she was sitting under a few minutes prior.

"Hey, Matty," she said, kicking up a little water to splash him and get his attention as he was distracted by searching under rocks for creatures.

"Hey! What was that for?" Matty exclaimed, sounding more like a child than he had before.

"Sorry. I just wanted to ask you something. Have you ever climbed that tree?"

A sly smile slid across Matty's face. "No, but I've always wanted to."

"Me too, but I've never wanted to do it alone...."

"C'mon, then! Let's climb all the way to the top, and then I'll tell you all of my secrets."

With that, Matty and Laila ran off to the big oak tree that was decades and decades older than they were. Their feet were still wet and they didn't want to put on their shoes and socks, so they climbed the tree barefoot ignoring the possibility of getting splinters.

Many good, low branches made it not too difficult to climb. Usually, Laila was afraid of heights, but there was something so exciting about climbing that tree for the first time with Matty that made her push the acrophobia out of her mind.

Finally, they reached the highest branch that they were sure could support both of their weights. They sat straddled on the branch facing each other hidden in the big, green leaves, and took deep gulps of fresh air in to catch their breath.

Matty laughed and Laila laughed too because she couldn't get over the sound of his childish giggle.

"What's so funny?" Laila asked.

"Nothing. It's just that it's funny to look down on everybody. They're so innocent and unsuspecting of everything that is going on to happen in the next decade," Matty stated matter-of-factly.

"That's true, I suppose. You know, I've always wondered if we knew our future whether or not we would continue you on," Laila said.

"That's a very philosophical thought for a nine-year-old," Matty observed. "Very sullen, too."

"It's terrible to say, but sometimes I think we're all living off hope in some way and that hope never seems to come through. Things never seem to get all the much better for some people. I mean I'm pretty happy with my life, but for some others... I don't know. Do you get what I'm saying?"

Matty looked Laila in the eyes and got serious, "Now you know why I said I wasn't excited for college."

Laila nodded her head. "I guess that makes sense, but just like all of those people down there don't know what is ahead of them in the next decade neither do you. I'm sure none of them would have guessed the United States would have a reality TV star for president, so anything can happen. I'm already excited for the twenties. I mean, you'll turn twenty in 2020, that's very auspicious. I have a feeling big Gatsby-like parties will come back into fashion."

Matty shook his head and smirked, "I hope you're right, Laila."

Matty didn't seem convinced that there was reason to be hopeful and Laila felt bad for bringing up the topic in the first place, so she decided to change the subject. "Now that we've reached the top of the tree and caught our breath, what are all those secrets you were going to tell me?"

"Oh, those," Matty teased, "I don't think you'd be interested in them," he said sarcastically with a dramatic shrug and sigh.

Laila kicked his dangling foot with hers, and Matty almost lost his balance.

"Oops!" Laila said because she was not expecting Matty to teeter from her playful kick.

"I see how it is," Matty laughed, "You're trying to force those secrets out of me, aren't you, Laila?"

"No," Laila responded defensively, "But you did bring me into this crazy- whatever it is, without my full knowledge, so I do think you owe me some information."

Matty nodded in reluctant agreement. "I guess that's fair. What do you want to know?"

Laila thought for a moment. There was so much she wanted to know she didn't know where to start. She decided to ask him the first question to pop into her mind, "What was that drug that we took?"

"I figured you would ask that," Matty said, "It's called effugium."

"Ok, but what *is* effugium?" Laila insisted. She needed to know whether she took something highly dangerous and illegal or if she had taken something harmless and permissible.

"Well, it's an experimental drug, not on the market yet."

"Matty! You told me that they were totally normal. I knew I shouldn't have trusted you," Laila exclaimed.

Matty moved his hand over Laila's mouth which served only to frustrate her. "Shhh… they can't know we're just visiting," he said referencing the younger versions of our friends and family below us, "We have to act convincingly enough like children so that they don't become suspicious."

Matty lifted his hand from Laila's mouth. "Fine, but you need to tell me more about what I ingested."

Matty sighed. "For a while now, I would get these panic attacks. I'd feel like nobody liked me and that everything in the world was wrong. I would go from feeling like the most confident, egotistical kid to feeling like I didn't want to be alive anymore."

Laila was surprised by Matty's words. They were never close growing up, but Laila was still shocked that Matty could have been going through all of that, and she never noticed a thing. Laila nodded reassuringly to encourage Matty to continue.

"And so, my parents took me to more doctors, psychiatrists, psychologists, and counselors than you could count. I went to weekly counseling sessions and I was on and off a variety of prescription medications that they thought would make me feel better, but for some reason, the peace never lasted and I wasn't happy for long."

"Why?" Laila asked bluntly. She knew the question was rude and a little uncalled for, but she really wanted to know why this boy who seemed to have it all could be so messed up on the inside.

Matty shook his head, "I don't know, Laila. I just don't know. If I did, I would do whatever it took to fix it. Trust me. I feel guilty every day for being depressed. My parents have given me so much throughout the years and now this is how I pay them back."

Laila reached over and patted Matty's hand. "Don't say that. I'm sure your parents just want to do whatever they can to help you. It-it's not your fault, Matty."

Matty's eyes started to water up, but he wiped them quickly with the back of his hand.

"Anyway," he said, getting back to the first question Laila had asked, "the effugium, is a new medication they're testing for people's depression when it doesn't get better after normal treatment. It's passed through all of the safety tests though, so don't worry about that. I wouldn't give you anything that I thought could harm you."

Laila was feeling a bit more relaxed and relieved now, "Matty, you know you shouldn't have shared your medication with me."

Matty looked over at the other children who were now in the middle of a three-legged race. "I know," he said, his eyes getting a little hazy, "It's just that, it makes me feel a lot better and it's like an amazing secret that only I know about, and well now you, of course. But trust me, Laila. I've been taking these for five days, now and I've had no side effects. I wouldn't let you have them if I thought they were going to hurt you. I only want you to be happy."

Laila pondered what Matty had said for a moment. This effugium could be harmful to her, she thought even if Matty didn't think so. Laila made a vow to herself in her head that she would never take one again, but she didn't want to upset Matty at the moment so she asked him another question.

"Who else is a part of this clinical study?"

"Only thirty others across the country."

"So, it is legal?" Laila asked just to be sure.

"Well, yes, but not for you, technically. You didn't sign all of the waivers and special paperwork," Matty admitted, "But, please, trust me, no one's going to find out. It's fine."

Laila took a deep breath in. She wondered how her ordinary self got mixed-up in this strange, medically-induced wonderland.

"Alright," Laila agreed. "Do you know if the, erm… the other guinea pigs, patients are experiencing this as well?"

Matty hesitated. "I don't know, really. You see I'm not telling them exactly what is happening because, well, I'm afraid that if I do they'll take the pills away from me and I don't want that to happen. Instead, I just tell them the medication helps me manage my self-destructive thoughts and makes me less irritable."

"I see…" Laila said taking a moment to process whether Matty was insane or she was or possibly both. "Wait, where are we *really* right now?"

Matty had to think about his question. "We are in two places at once, at least that's what I believe. We feel everything in this world, but our bodies are still lying on my bed fast asleep. I like to call it escaping."

"So, when are we going to wake up?"

"That's the cool part," Matty smiled, "we get to decide."

"I guess we shouldn't stay too long, then. My mother's going to be wondering where I am and maybe she's called or texted me and is worried about me…" Laila droned on.

"Oh, Laila, don't ruin the fun yet. We've only been here a half an hour, I'd say. Don't you want to say hello to your past mom before we have to face the reality of December 20, 2017, again?"

"Alright," Laila relented. In all truth, she was enjoying herself. Getting to re-experience a warm summer's day from her childhood was thrilling and calming all at the same time. It was much more fun than being buried under her bedsheets scrolling through Instagram after school.

"Good!" Matty cheered. "When you want to go, just let me know. All we have to do is think about how much we miss the reality we left and we'll be back before you know it."

"This feels like a messed-up version of a Disney movie," Laila chuckled remembering how Peter Pan and Wendy used to think happy thoughts to fly to Neverland.

"Perhaps, but right now it doesn't feel so wrong to me," Matty shrugged.

After that, Laila and Matty proceeded to carefully climb down the tree. Laila might have slipped if it wasn't for the one time Matty reached down and grabbed her hand so that she could regain her balance and grip.

Once they were back on land with their feet firmly placed in the soft grass they put their sneakers on and separately ran over to reunite with their long-lost family.

Laila ran into her mother's arms and cherished the warm feeling of her hug. She told her mother how she had climbed the oak tree with Matty. Laila's heart soared when her mother told her how proud she was of her and boasted to Laila's father who was standing nearby.

For a moment, Laila thought she might want to stay there forever and never return to reality. It was nice to see her parents looking and acting more youthful again. Plus, she had missed how affectionate they were around her when she was younger.

Then, Laila remembered the triplets. She wanted to go back and see them. Laila wanted to give Charlotte a hug and tell her that she was her favorite sister. (Charlotte always thought that this was a great compliment, until age seven when she realized it was a paradox because Charlotte was Laila's only sister.)

Laila gave her parents each one last hug before running off to find Matty. He was waiting by the creek for her. His brown eyes seemed to be mesmerized by the bubbling, rushing water. He was sitting perfectly still. He had just the slightest grin on his face. Laila didn't think she had ever seen him like that before, so quiet and at peace.

Laila tapped him on the shoulder. Matty looked up at her and motioned for her to sit down next to him.

"I'm ready to go," she whispered.

Matty glanced over at Laila with said resignation. "If we have to," he said, "Just close your eyes and start imagining the good things waiting for you when we return back. I'll do the same. One of us might get back first. If you wake up and I'm still there asleep you'll know that I'm still here, but don't worry. I'll eventually make it back home."

Laila agreed. She felt a little nervous and said a quick, quiet prayer hoping that it would work.

Laila closed her eyes and thought about stopping on the way home for cupcakes to make the triplets smile, the snowstorm predicted to come in a couple of days, and her cozy bed waiting for her at home.

Before Laila knew it, she was back in Matty's room. She sat up and saw that Matty was still asleep or still in the escape, as he had called it.

Laila looked out his window again and admired the view. Someday, she thought she would like to hike on that mountain again with Matty. He seemed to be the perfect person to take on adventures.

Matty stirred a few minutes later and woke up. He rubbed his eyes and got out of bed a little more groggily than Laila had.

"Good morning," Laila kidded. For some reason, Laila was in a very good mood despite just having the strangest experience of her seventeen years.

Matty laughed good-naturedly and joined Laila by the window. They gazed out in silence together for a moment. Then Matty said simply, "Thank you for coming with me, Laila."

Without looking back at him Laila reciprocated his gratitude, "Thanks for having me, Matty."

"Do you think you'd like me to show you other places as well sometime?" Matty asked while looking out at the setting sun on the gray mountain peak shrouded with clouds.

This time Laila turned to him and looked at his teenage face until he looked back at her.

"Yes," Laila said, biting her lip. Not long ago she had vowed to herself that she wasn't going to take effugium another time, but now she felt almost desperate to take one of those pills again. Laila wanted to see happy places, people, and times with Matty again so badly, but she didn't want to let on how great her longing was.

A wide grin spread across Matty's face, "That's what I was hoping you would say," he said.

Laila blushed and grabbed her phone and coat from his nightstand.

"It's almost four o'clock. I'd better be on my way," Laila announced.

"Should we do this again, tomorrow?" Matty asked with a raised eyebrow. Laila could hear the hope in his voice and she knew that if she declined his offer Matty would feel bad for himself, so she agreed. Of course, she was hoping he would offer anyway.

"Yes," Laila said.

"Great," Matty said and the two just stood there staring out the window in silence for a long time.

"I'll show myself out," Laila said when it seemed as though Matty wasn't going to walk her to the door.

"Goodbye, Laila. I'll see ya tomorrow," Matty said happily his attention still partially on the view outside his window.

"Goodbye," Laila said quietly.

Laila showed herself out and drove home, remembering to stop at the bakery for special cupcakes on the way.

When Laila arrived home for the first time in a while she was truly looking forward to seeing her family. She gave them each a big hug and even volunteered to help the triplets with their homework while her mother made spaghetti and meatballs.

Laila helped her mom with the dishes that evening while her dad put the little ones to bed. Laila thought it was nice to have some time with her mother alone.

Even though Laila's mother wasn't working as many hours anymore at the studio, Laila could tell she was exhausted.

"Hey, Mom…" Laila asked, drying off a sippy cup that her brother was way too old to be using but way too klutzy to not be using.

"Yeah, baby," Laila's mother replied, sending a warm wave through Laila's body. Laila loved when her mom called her sweet names which she rarely did since Laila became a teenager and her mother had to focus on the real babies.

"Ummm… what do you think Matty's family is like?" Laila mumbled.

"Laila, you know his parents. They're at church every Sunday. They sit a few pews behind us," Laila's mother answered.

She was confused by Laila's question which she regarded as too odd to entertain.

"It's just that I wonder about Matty is all," Laila spoke softly.

"What about Matty?" Laila's mother asked.

"Nothing. I just wonder if maybe he's not as happy as everyone assumes he is," Laila explained.

Laila's mother shook her head. She didn't understand what Laila was talking about. Of course, she wouldn't because she had never seen that side of Matty Laila had. "What are you talking about? Matty's happy. He's got parents that want the best for him, acceptances into amazing schools, he's good-looking…. Why wouldn't he be happy?"

Laila frowned. She was frustrated because there were so many things she couldn't say to her mother, but if she could it would have made things make sense. "Well, you know those things don't make you happy. Right, Mom?" Laila said defensively.

"Laila you're just being cynical. You're imagining things that aren't there," Laila's mother shot back at her.

"Fine. Whatever," Laila realized she shouldn't have even brought the subject up.

The rest of the night, Laila spent trying to enjoy being with her mother and father. Part of her wanted to tell them what had happened that afternoon, but, of course, she knew she absolutely could not. There was no way they would understand and they would think she was lying to get attention. Instead, Laila kept her lovely little secret to herself.

8 WINTER WONDERLAND

Matty woke up late the next morning. He usually didn't sleep in, but something about having the house to himself made him feel like it.

Matty thought about his escape with Laila the day before. He had not expected them to experience the same escape at the same time. It was a pleasant surprise. Now, Matty would barely want to take effugium without Laila by his side. It was so much more fun to have someone else from the present to interact with.

After pouring himself a bowl of cereal and sitting down on his mother's white couch, Matty thought about what he should say to Laila. He felt kind of bad for not chatting with her properly the day before. Matty figured Laila probably thought he was off his rocker. Which he was the day before.

Matty decided he should ask her to do something like normal friends do instead of just inviting her over to take some of his experimental medication again. Matty pulled out his phone and texted Laila.

<<Hey, Laila. Want to play video games over at my house this afternoon?

Video games? Is that a code?>>

<<Only if you want it to be.

I'll ask my mom and see if I can drive over.>>

I'll be over in twenty minutes. Need to help the triplets get ready for a bday party first.>>

"Mom, is it alright if I go to a friend's house this afternoon?" Laila asked as she tied Charlotte's shoes.

"Yeah, I guess so," Laila's mother said while zipping up Aaron's coat. She was excited for her daughter who rarely met with peers outside of school. "Who's the friend?"

"Oh, um... it's Matty," Laila said. She knew there was no point in lying, but she wanted to because Laila didn't know what her mother would make of the truth after Laila had been asking her strange questions about Matty the day before.

"Ben, please put the legos down. For the last time I'm telling you it's time to get ready for your friend's party," Mrs. Jennings yelled into the other room. Laila rolled her eyes. It was difficult to have an uninterrupted conversation.

Laila started to walk away taking her mother's distraction as approval.

"Wait, Laila," she called, "since when have you and Matty been friends?" Laila's mother asked, looking her daughter in the eye.

Laila turned pale. She didn't know how to answer the question. Since yesterday? Since forever? Were they even friends?

"We're lab partners this semester. Biology, you know," Laila lied, "And we're in the same economics and Spanish classes and we have to talk a lot so we became friends."

Laila's mother turned to help Ben find his mittens while Laila finished her explanation. Maybe because she wasn't paying much attention or maybe because Laila's story was good, she bought it.

"Alright, just be safe. Don't do anything Daddy and I wouldn't be proud of and be home before dinner. Grandma's stopping over at 6:30 to eat with us."

"Thanks, Mom. I will," Laila beamed grabbing her coat and car keys.

"Going out already?" Mom asked, lacing up her own boots.

"Yep," Laila said, popping the p. "See ya later," she waved before rushing out the door.

Laila hopped in the car and didn't even worry about music. She was too preoccupied with thoughts of what might happen at Matty's. It was all so surreal and Laila could barely believe she got to be a part of it.

Laila knew that she really shouldn't have been entertaining Matty and his sharing of drugs and split personality, but something about it felt right. Kind of like when someone gets their first boyfriend or girlfriend and instantly starts making wedding plans.

What Laila had yet to acknowledge consciously was that she liked Matty. Laila "like, liked" Matty; she just didn't know it yet. In her mind, she told herself they were only friends and would never be more than that, but soon enough her heart would get involved.

Laila walked up to Matty's house and rang his doorbell. He opened it still in his pyjamas with ruffled hair.

"Thanks for having me over," Laila said politely as he let her in.

"Thanks for coming. I was kind of worried I might have scared you away yesterday," Matty admitted as he gestured for her to sit down on the couch with him.

"I was kind of confused," Laila said while slipping her coat off.

"I know," Matty nodded, "I'm sorry I didn't explain it to you better. It's just kind of hard to put into words. And I haven't been doing it that long myself, and now I don't really know much more than you do."

"That's okay. I guess it's just kind of strange seeing you outside of school or work. You just act so differently."

"Well, I guess that's because I'm not like you, Laila. I can't just be who I am. That's just not how it works for me. You're lucky that you feel like you can be exactly you wherever you go, around whoever you meet, but I don't. I think that's a pretty normal thing. I don't know."

"It's called being honest with yourself, I think," Laila wondered out loud.

"No, I think it's called self-assuredness."

"So, video games…" Laila said changing the subject. She wasn't going to let Matty wallow in his angst.

"Oh, yeah, video games. I thought that maybe you'd actually like to hang out properly because, you know, I do honestly want to be friends with you, Laila."

"Well, what have you got?" Laila chuckled.

Matty sprawled out on the floor and pulled out a chest with rows of video game cases neatly stacked, controllers, and accessories.

"You've got everything there, don't you?"

"Not everything, but enough to entertain myself. What kind of things do you like? There's the new *Call of Duty World War II* if you're into that. There's all the new Nintendo Switch stuff my mom got for me. Fifa and all the sports games for Playstation are in this drawer…"

"What's this?" Laila asked, pulling out the original *Just Dance.*

"Please not that. My cousins got it for me years ago. We used to play it on holidays. My aunt wanted us to be more active. Now it just sits in there and collects dust," Matty whined.

"You said I could pick!" Laila protested.

Matty groaned. "Do you have to pick this one?"

"Yes. I hate sports and I don't want to shoot soldiers either."

"Fine," Matty yielded as he opened the case and slid the disc into his Wii console.

Laila and Matty grabbed the controllers and waited for the game to load. Matty demanded that he should get to be player one because Laila got to pick the game which she allowed.

The two played for a while. At first, Matty was not very enthusiastic but after losing a couple of rounds he put in the effort to try and beat Laila. She didn't care about winning or losing. She was just glad to be having fun with Matty.

After they had danced to all of their favorite songs in the game, Matty insisted that Laila challenge him in *MarioKart*. Laila had played that game before so she thought she might have a chance of competing with Matty, but she was wrong. Matty had played every course so many times that he had every twist in the CGI roads memorized, not to mention the shortcuts and glitches.

Around the time Laila fell into the abyss that surrounds Rainbow Road for the tenth time, they decided to call it quits on video games for a little while.

Matty decided it was be a good time to give Laila an official tour of his house, so he walked her around and showed her where his parents hid Christmas parents, the water heater he used to be scared of, and the sunroom where the cats spent all day napping. Matty showed Laila the boring stuff too, but she didn't mind. Laila admired the house and wished that someday she could live in one like it.

Eventually, they reached Matty's bedroom which was the last stop on the tour and the most thorough. Matty showed Laila every soccer trophy, explained every photo, and revealed his secret collection of Taylor Swift albums.

Once Matty had finally finished his ultimate show-and-tell speech, Laila popped the question she had been waiting all afternoon to ask, "Can we escape again?"

"Okay," Matty said sitting down on the left side of his bed, "but, there is something I need to make sure you understand."

Laila took a seat next to him. Both of their feet dangled from the side of the mattress. She nodded for him to continue.

"Things won't be like they were yesterday. As far as I can tell, you can never escape to the same moment more than once," Matty explained.

"That's alright," Laila said, eager to get on with it.

Matty went on, "And you need to realize it might not be a moment from *your* lifetime."

Laila didn't know if she was comfortable with escaping to a moment outside of her lifetime, but she didn't say anything.

Matty laughed, "Don't be so worried," he said, noticing her hesitant expression, "It won't be unfamiliar. It might just be a place you haven't seen before with your eyes or a place your feet haven't walked yet."

"I can't understand, but I'm willing to try anyway."

"You don't have to give it another go if you don't want to," Matty offered one last time.

Laila shook her head, "No, I like adventure," she smiled with a false display of confidence.

Matty grinned in giddy approval, "I like you, Laila," he said reaching into his bedside drawer for two effugium pills, "you're different. You are so Laila."

"Is that a compliment?"

"I don't know," Matty said with a cocky smile before swallowing the pill.

Matty laid back with his feet dangling on the side of the bed and eyes closed. Laila watched as the muscles in his body seemed to relax and a slight grin appeared on his face. For a moment, Laila looked down at him and studied the mysterious boy. She couldn't make much sense of him, but she had a sinking feeling he'd never leave her heart or mind all of the days of her life.

Laila laid the chalky pill on her tongue and took a sip of water from the bottle he had on his nightstand. She closed her eyes and slowly reclined her body onto Matty's firm mattress. Laila enjoyed feeling warm, peaceful, and tired before arriving in the escape.

On this day when Laila opened her eyes, she found herself in a bed that felt not too different from the one Matty and she were laying in back home.

Laila looked around. The room was dark and small. There was a person beside her. He was turned the other direction and Laila thought he might be sleeping. She pushed the covers off that were only keeping her slightly warm and realized then that it was a patchwork quilt she had woken under.

A dim light illuminated the room just enough so that Laila was able to walk and roughly guess the dimensions of the room and the furniture it contained.

Laila turned in her place and took in the surroundings. The walls were made of thick, horizontal wooden logs stacked up on top of each other with a few inches of lighter-colored material in between. Laila had never been in a log cabin before, but from the drawings she had seen in picture books she assumed she was in one.

On the right side of the room, there was a rather small chest of drawers, and adjacent to it was a coat rack that seemed to be holding a coat or two. On the left side of the room, there was a small mirror hanging from the wall and a portrait of an older couple.

Laila wondered if she was embodying the wife in the portrait. She touched her face. No, it felt smooth, soft, and young. Laila could feel that she was standing just about as tall as she did in her real body. She looked down at her arms and she recognized them as her own. Everything about her body seemed very much like herself, but Laila knew wherever she was she hadn't been before.

The man in the bed started to stir and Laila became frightened. She didn't know who the man was and she didn't know how to act around him. Laila wondered if she was supposed to be his wife in this delusional world and she began to regret taking effugium for the second time.

Then, the man sat up in the bed and rubbed his eyes. Laila couldn't help but notice that he looked muscular and strong. He had a little stubble around his chin, Laila believed, and was dressed in an old-fashioned nightshirt.

"Laila?" the man asked cautiously. Laila recognized his voice and a wave of relief washed over her.

"Matty?" she cried out excitedly.

He laughed. "Where are we?"

"I- I don't know Matty, but we're certainly not in the modern era," Laila stuttered before crawling back in bed. Laila sat with her back against the headboard and pulled the quilt up to her neck to stay warm.

"It's so cold," Matty said through chattering teeth.

"Yeah," Laila agreed, "This isn't quite as much fun as the Fourth of July picnic."

"No, but that's just how it goes. You don't get to pick where you escape to. You just have to be happy that you were lucky enough to escape."

"What shall we do?" Laila asked.

"Shall?" Matty laughed giving Laila a playful push on the shoulder. "I've never heard you use that word before."

Laila shrugged. "It just sort of felt right," Laila explained, slightly embarrassed.

"That's okay," Matty said, reassuring her. "I think that it's best to act the part when you're around other people in these escapes. That way, they don't become suspicious."

"Matty," Laila started nervously, "What would happen if someone in one of these places found out we weren't a part of their world?"

At this point, the sun was almost risen and Laila could see the features of Matty's face a little more clearly.

After a moment of consideration, he said, "I'm not sure. I suppose it would depend on the person. If we lived in Salem during the witch trials we would surely be burned at the stake."

Matty and Laila both laughed at that, but it was fake laughter because they were both now presently afraid of dying in an escape.

"What would you do if you ran into someone in real life and they told you they were in an escape, that they weren't really who you thought they were?" Matty asked, suddenly.

"Hmmm... well, I'd probably never believe them. How could anyone believe something as magical as this is real?"

"You're probably right. That's why I couldn't just tell you about them, I had to show you," Matty explained lying back down on the bed and snuggling into the quilt in a desperate attempt to ward off the cold.

Laila curled into herself beside him. They lay facing opposite directions. They were both freezing.

"Why did you show me?" Laila asked impulsively. It was the first time the question ever popped into her head and suddenly she was desperate to know the answer.

"I wanted someone else to talk to about it. I wanted to make sure I wasn't crazy and you're the only person I know who I thought would appreciate escaping," Matty said simply. "Plus, it's more fun with you. Imagine waking up in this cabin alone. It would be alright, I guess, but in most situations, it's better to wake up with someone by your side," he added.

Matty's words sent butterflies to Laila's stomach. Laila hadn't made the conscious connection that he preferred being with her than being alone. As an introvert, Laila knew what a compliment that was.

"I like escaping with you," Laila blurted out without thinking. It was true, but Laila couldn't understand why she verbalized it. After all, she was afraid of saying anything that would boost Matty's ego.

"I'm glad you do. I thought you would. You know we've never been good friends in the real world. But somehow I just knew you would like this. We're very different, you know, but in the deepest, truest ways we're the same."

Laila loved the way Matty said in the deepest, truest ways. He seemed honest about it.

"The deepest, truest ways," Laila repeated Matty subconsciously under her breath.

"Yes, you know like in your heart and stuff like that," Matty said, sounding more teenagery and less poetic than he had moments before.

"Maybe," Laila said.

"Like we both see the world unlike everybody else. When I look in your blue eyes, Laila, I can tell you feel both the deep sadness of humanity and the deep joy all at once. I can tell you intrinsically love people but grow more frustrated with them every day. I can tell that you love yourself enough that being alone doesn't hurt you. And Laila I want to be like that."

Laila started to shake at what Matty had said. It was true, every word of it. But Laila couldn't understand how he knew those things about her. After reflecting upon Matty's words for a moment she accepted them as an accurate description of her experience, although she had never known those things about herself before, at least not in her conscious mind.

"You are right, Matty," Laila said, turning in the bed to face him. It was then that she noticed Matty wasn't the same-bodied boy she went to school with. There was hardly a trace of boyishness on his face in this escape. There were even some wrinkles on his forehead, but other things had improved. His skin was clearer and his jawline was noticeably more prominent. Every line on his face seemed less curved and less soft and sharper.

Matty grinned. "I know," he chuckled a bit arrogantly in a way that reminded Laila of the boy from her hometown. His smile hadn't changed at all. Laila figured smiles must not change.

For a second or two, Laila and Matty just looked into each other's eyes. It wasn't a long amount of time, but to Laila, it felt like an eternity. It was like they were seeing each other for the first time. Laila realized that Matty was much purer and more innocent and so much kinder than she thought. Matty felt Laila too and she was exactly the goodness he thought she was.

Then, something strange happened. Laila saw herself in Matty's eyes, first reflected, and then inside of Matty like she had become a part of him.

The moment of sincerity and serenity was interrupted by the sound of a rooster crowing from outside.

"Maybe we should get up and explore," Matty suggested.

"Sure," Laila smiled swiftly getting up from the bed, bracing herself for the cool, biting air while Matty stayed under the quilt for a minute longer. Laila walked over to the window to peer out of what seemed like an endless meadow of snow-covered hills.

"So, where do you think we are exactly?" she asked.

"Could be anywhere, really," Matty said distractedly, "It seems like sometime around the Civil War, give or take a decade or two. I'm not too into history to know for sure."

"It doesn't matter, I guess. It seems like we're alone out here, wherever we are," Laila said, still looking out at the horizon as the bright winter's sun reflected off the shiny, white snow making the landscape look like heaven.

"I wouldn't speak so soon. There could be children in this house," Matty mused, pulling out a pair of woolen trousers and flannel from the chest of drawers for himself along with a woolen skirt and blouse Laila assumed he intended for her. "If I had to say by looking at the two of us, I would say that we're in our late twenties and married."

Laila was embarrassed at what Matty was implying. "What you're saying, then, is that this is an alternate reality, a parallel universe?"

"You could describe an escape like this that way, I believe," Matty agreed, pulling his trousers on underneath his nightshirt. Laila turned away as he pulled his pyjamas off and replaced them with the red and green, plaid flannel.

"You could have looked," Matty joked. "I was only missing my shirt for a second."

"I didn't want to," Laila lied. She picked up the clothing he had laid aside for her and looked at it. Laila realized it was her turn to change out of the white, cotton nightgown into the dreaded skirt and blouse. Unlike Matty, she couldn't change and retain her modesty at the same time.

Laila looked over at Matty expectantly. He shortly figured out that Laila wanted him to give her some privacy.

"Oh, I'll wait for you in the next room," he said after making his realization.

Laila nodded, "Okay."

After Matty left the bedroom, she slipped off the nightgown and put on the day clothes with uncertainty. Laila had never worn anything like this before. She looked at herself in the small mirror.

Laila looked different. Her cheeks weren't as round as she was used to, and her braided hair was significantly longer. Like Matty, Laila's skin had cleared up and there were a few wrinkles by her eyes.

Laila smiled at the woman in the mirror. She was proud of how she had grown, at least in this escape, from a girl to a lady. She knew that she would remember this moment for a long time whenever she thought about her future.

Then, Laila turned and practically skipped out to Matty. As she pushed open the curtain that separated the bedroom from the rest of the house, Laila saw Matty there waiting for her. He was sitting at a rather primitively constructed table looking through an old copy of Charles Dickens' *A Christmas Carol*.

"No kids," Matty said as Laila explored the kitchen, dining, and living area that made up the only other room in the house. Laila was relieved because she didn't want to spend the rest of the escape babysitting.

"I saw that there were two sets of snowshoes outside," Matty mentioned putting the book aside.

"Let's go, then. This cabin's cute but much too boring," Laila said excitedly.

So, they put on whatever coats, mittens, hats, scarves, and boots they could find. Then, they stepped outside into the bright sun and helped each other lace up the snowshoes.

Together, Matty and Laila walked around the snow-covered hills while periodically stopping to throw a few snowballs.

Laila remembered one of her favorite activities from her childhood, making snow angels and she asked Matty to make some with her. Matty counted to three and they fell back into the snow at the same time. It didn't work out like Laila had imagined though. They both just became buried in the two feet of snow.

Matty and Laila traveled further and further away from the log cabin and into the prairie hoping to find something interesting. Laila sang Christmas carols as they hiked to make things more fun, she said.

They reached a point where the earth sloped down ahead of them steeply. They were standing at the top of one of the longest, steepest hills they had ever seen.

"Oh look! I wish we had a sled," Laila exclaimed.

"I know, this is the best sledding hill ever."

Laila and Matty gazed down at the hill longingly for a moment until Matty piped up.

"Well, it's not as deep here. The snow has drifted to the bottom of the hill...."

"Yeah."

"So, what I'm thinking is we could roll down the hill."

"Yes!" Laila shouted and then proceeded to lay down on her back. Matty did the same a few feet away from her.

"Ready?" Matty hollered.

"Ready!"

"Alright, go!" Then, the race began. Matty and Laila both started as rolling as fast as they could down the white hill making sure to cover their faces with their hands.

It was an exhilarating feeling. Both Laila and Matty laughed and screamed as they got dizzier by the minute.

Laila felt so free although she had lost control of her body due to the momentum she had picked up. Then, suddenly Laila felt a sharp pain shoot through her ankle. It hurt worse than anything

Laila had felt before. She started to cry. She tried to stop herself from rolling down the hill, but she couldn't.

Matty heard Laila when she shouted in pain. He knew something was wrong. Matty spread his arms out and pushed his feet as hard as he could into the snow. He had stopped himself just before reaching the end of the hill.

Matty pushed himself up onto his knees. He was so dizzy; his vision was blurred. He spotted Laila lying some twenty feet away from him. Matty ran toward her on unsteady legs.

"Laila, what happened? Are you okay?" he called out.

"No," she groaned through sobs. "My foot or my ankle- I don't know which. It hurts so bad. I think I sprained or broke it or something," she cried as he reached her.

Matty felt his heart start to beat faster and a sick feeling came to his stomach. It was all his fault. He shouldn't have suggested that they roll down the hill. Now, Laila was hurt. "Alright, alright. It's going to be okay. I'll call-" Matty stopped himself. There was no one to call. Even if there was, he didn't have a phone. He didn't have anything.

Matty looked in Laila's eyes as she lay on her back. They were filled with tears and the tears were beginning to freeze on her rosy cheeks.

"We have to go back. We have to leave the escape. There's nothing else we can do," Matty said as calmly as he could while holding her hands to comfort her.

"No, I'm not ready. What if we get back and it's not healed. I want to stay."

"Laila, you can't walk. Can you?"

"I can try," Laila mumbled weakly. Laila pushed herself up and Matty helped her stand by supporting her weight. When Laila put her left foot firmly down a fresh set of tears came falling down her face while she sobbed loudly a few more times.

"Shh, shh…" Matty said sweetly, rubbing her back. "It's going to be okay," he whispered into her ear, letting her lean onto him.

"I'm sorry," Laila stuttered.

"No, it's okay. It's not your fault. It's mine. I just don't know what to do. That's all." Matty had never comforted someone like this before, but somehow it came naturally.

"I want to go back to the cabin," Laila sniffled resting her head on Matty's shoulder.

"Are you sure you don't just want to think about home and everything good waiting for you there? Then in the blink of an eye, we'll be back in my room, safe and sound."

Laila didn't say anything. "Or I guess I could try carrying you back?" Matty proposed.

"Could you?" Laila said nodding her head.

"I'll try for you, okay," Matty nodded. Then, he helped set her down into the snow gently for a minute while he ran up the hill to put his snowshoes back on. He came back down for her and kneeled down so she could climb onto his back. Matty stood up slowly but realized quickly that he was stronger than his normal self in this escape. Carrying Laila to the cabin piggy-back style would be easier than he thought.

"Are you okay, up there?" Matty asked.

"I'm good. Are you?" Laila replied.

"Yup. Don't worry. We'll make it back."

Matty started up the hill and step-by-step he made it to the top with Laila clinging on to him the whole time. A few minutes into their walk, Laila stopped crying which signaled to Matty that there probably weren't any broken bones. It was likely a sprain.

"How's it feeling?" Matty asked.

"It hurts," Laila stated. "But it's not unbearable."

"When we get back, we can put some snow on it. You know it will kind of be like icing it."

"Ok," Laila sighed. She hoped Matty wasn't getting too tired carrying her, but she kind of enjoyed being carried except for the throbbing pain radiating from her ankle.

"Why were you so insistent on staying in the escape?" Matty wondered as they neared the cabin.

"I was having too much fun. I didn't want it to end just yet."

"Even with a sprained ankle?" Matty laughed.

"Yeah, even with a sprained ankle."

When they reached the cabin, Laila took off her coat, mittens, and hat and sat down at the table with the help of Matty. After Matty made a fire he helped Laila gently slip off the boot and sock from her left foot. Laila winced as Matty pulled up an extra chair for Laila to elevate her foot on.

All around Laila's ankle was blue turning black. Matty cringed when he saw how swollen it was.

"Is it that bad?" Laila frowned.

"It'll be okay, well at least it'll be okay whenever we leave this escape. I don't think it's going to get much better until then. But I'll grab some snow to put on it to numb the pain for now," Matty said. Then, he went just outside the door and made four or five snowballs. Matty took the snow inside and patted it down around Laila's ankle like he did at the beach with wet sand on his cousins' feet.

"Thanks. That feels good," Laila smiled gratefully.

"You're welcome," Matty nodded. They spent the next hour sipping hot cocoa from tin cups, staying warm under quilts, and listening to each other take turns reading *A Christmas Carol* in theatrical voices. Laila made it a game whoever could listen to the most pages without laughing won. Neither won because they were both so bad at the game.

"Matty," Laila yawned, "I think I'm ready to go home now. My parents will be expecting me soon."

"Me too," Matty agreed. "You know what to do. I'll see you back home," he promised.

With that, Matty and Laila closed their eyes. Matty thought about ordering a pizza and binge-watching *The Office*. Laila thought about being able to run on both feet without pain and having dinner with her grandmother.

And then, like a flash of lightning, Laila and Matty opened their eyes and found themselves laying horizontally on Matty's bed with their feet dangling off the side.

"That was wild!" Laila said, jumping off the bed.

"Really wild- in a good way," Matty grinned.

Laila checked the time on Matty's clock. Her eyes grew wide. "I got to go. My Grandma's supposed to be coming over for dinner in ten minutes."

"You'd better hurry, then. I'll walk you out."

9 PIRATES

Matty's parents returned home on Sunday morning. His mother was worried. She hadn't left Matty alone for that long since he started his downward spiral. She had called and texted many times throughout the weekend to check in on Matty, but he hadn't always answered. Maybe he was just being a normal teenager, she thought, but fear still held her tight.

To his parents' surprise, Matty was in an excellent mood when they arrived home. He was up and dressed and listening to music through the stereo instead of through his earbuds. And it wasn't the sad kind of music he liked; it was happy music his parents liked.

"How was your weekend?" Matty's mother asked, handing her son a box of doughnut holes she had picked up.

"Really good, Mom," he said, kissing her on the cheek.

"Yeah? What did you do?"

"I had a friend over to play videos, ordered a pizza last night for myself, slept in. Not much."

"What friend?"

"Laila Jennings, you know her, right?" Matty said while popping a chocolate doughnut into his mouth.

"Yeah, I didn't know you were friends though."

"We are. Good friends."

"Oh, well I'm glad to hear it, then. Just no girls over when we're not home, anymore. Kay?" she smiled ruffling Matty's hair.

He rolled his eyes, "Whatever, Mom."

"Whatever, Matty," she said mimicking her son before he went for one of his habitual walks in the woods.

After he was out the door, Mr. and Mrs. Holt exchanged high-fives. It was the first time Matty had mentioned a girl and they considered it a milestone.

Meanwhile, over at the Jennings' house, Laila was anxiously awaiting a call from Matty. He told her he would ring her in the morning and now it was almost noon and he hadn't called.

Laila was beginning to become obsessed. Not just with the thought of escaping, but with the thought of Matty. He wasn't a perfect guy, but he had her captivated. His eyes, his insecurities, his laugh, his smile, his cocky attitude, and his soft soul- she was hooked on all of it. Laila had taken effugium, but she had become addicted to Matty.

"Why didn't you call earlier?" Laila demanded when Matty buzzed her quarter afternoon.

"Sorry, Laila. I was busy," he explained. He didn't understand her frustration because Matty wasn't addicted to Laila. He was just addicted to not being lonely.

"Oh, okay," Laila sighed.

"I don't think we can hang out today. My parents just got back, but don't worry I won't take effugium without you," Matty said from the forest he was wandering in.

"That's fine. We wouldn't want them to get suspicious, anyway. Going from never talking about each other to meeting up for hours every day."

"We can go over to my house again after school. There's a good two hours where I have the place to myself before my parents get home."

"Yeah that sounds good," Laila said excitedly.

"Ok, well see ya."

"See ya," Laila frowned before Matty hung up. She was disappointed the conversation had ended so quickly.

Laila spent the rest of the day in her little oasis of a bedroom. She tried to figure out Matty, but she couldn't. She tried to figure out why she liked him, but she couldn't. So, she wrote poems and songs. Laila wrote enough to fill an entire diary, but the words she wrote were too precious to be shared with anyone. Later that night, Laila snuck down to the basement where her parents kept a paper shredder and she shredded each page of her beautiful collection of art.

The next morning, Laila arrived at school eager to see Matty, but she was upset immediately. Laila wanted Matty to see her and notice her and talk to her. In a way, she felt closer to him than anyone else in the entire building, but apparently, he didn't feel the same way. Or maybe he did. Laila didn't know.

When Laila waved to him shyly in the hallway after the third period, all he could give Laila was a half-hearted grin before looking in the other direction. Laila gave him the benefit of the doubt and assumed maybe he was just tired, but later in Spanish class, he completely ignored her when she tried to say hello to him.

Laila wondered how Matty could be so insolent. She was frustrated and confused.

Part of Laila wanted to ditch Matty at the end of the day. She thought it would serve him right to be ignored, but in her heart, Laila knew she couldn't resist the curiosity she had to escape with him again.

Throughout the day, Laila tried to convince herself that Matty was a bad person for practically pretending she didn't exist while being over-the-top charismatic with others. Laila felt jealous because everyone else got the smiley Matty and she had to deal with the other not-so-smiley parts of Matty.

But then, Laila felt sort of bad for everyone else because even though they might have been getting a nicer, cleaner version of Matty, they weren't getting the real Matty, the hot mess Matty, the existential thinker, the one who believed in the unbelievable and carried her through the snow. Only Laila knew that side of Matty and she felt grateful for it.

So, Laila met Matty at his house after school.

"Hey," Matty smiled, swinging the door open.

"Hey," Laila said quietly without making eye contact. She walked in and sat down on the couch not bothering to take her coat off yet.

"Is something wrong?" Matty asked in a completely innocent voice which only served to irritate Laila further.

Laila groaned. "Well, I don't know," she said standing up so that she could get closer to eye level with Matty, "It's just that I thought we were, like, friends. I thought our escapes were good. I thought we changed over the weekend. Hanging out with you was kind of a big deal to me, but then, today you just acted like nothing had changed between you and me and it has, Matty. You can't act like things are the same because they aren't. They're just not, okay?" Laila could feel her face turning red. She couldn't understand why she was so offended by the way Matty had treated her. Normally, Laila couldn't care less if people gave her attention, but it was different with Matty.

Matty let out an exhausted sigh. "I didn't mean to hurt your feelings," he explained, "and you're right. Everything has changed, but we can't let that show. This is a secret. No one can know anything. If someone finds out we're friends, then they'll start to suspect we're more than friends, and they'll want to know more and more about us and somehow, someone will find out what we're doing. Then, we won't be able to do it anymore and that would be worse than never exchanging a smile in the stairwell."

"That's not fair," Laila pouted, "Plus, you could have at least given me a warning."

Matty was starting to feel bad, but his pride wouldn't let him show it. He shrugged unsympathetically, "I suppose you don't want to do this anymore."

Laila took a deep breath in. "Well, no..."

"Then, you're going to have to learn to play by my rules because it's my game," Matty declared.

Laila didn't like the way Matty was talking down to her, but she decided it would be better to keep her comments to herself, so she bit her lip instead.

"I'm sorry," he said, "I didn't mean to come off that way. Will you please escape with me, Laila?" Matty was being kind of sarcastic, but Laila accepted his apology anyway.

"I hate your rules," Laila said, crossing her arms.

"Come on, please, Laila," Matty begged.

"Fine," she huffed before following him to his bedroom where they laid down, took an effugium pill each, and closed their eyes.

In this escape, when Laila first opened her eyes, she was more nervous than comforted or thrilled.

She was sitting on a rough, wooden surface. The raggedy dress Laila was wearing was soaked through on the underside. The blue fabric stuck to her skin uncomfortably as a salty breeze blew the dress and her wild hair to one side and then the other. Laila tried to stand-up because she was feeling quite nauseous and wanted to find a place that would be better suited for throwing up. It was then that she realized her ankles were haphazardly tied together with rope.

Laila's hands were tied up too, but not to each other. She moved her finger and felt the hands of her fellow captive's move in response. The other's hands were slightly larger than Laila's and they were masculine, but they were equally as encrusted with dirt.

"Matty," Laila whispered, pushing her back against the rough, wooden pole behind her.

She felt her hand squeezed reassuringly, "Yes," the voice of seventeen-year-old Matty whispered back, "It's me, Laila."

Laila strained her neck to get a better view of the surroundings. To her right, there was a platform a few feet high with a large sail flying about it and a man in crude 17th century clothing standing at a wheel studying the horizon. To her left, Lalia noticed an even larger sail and an apparatus of nets, pulleys, and rigs. There were loud, strong, swearing men working by it.

Laila sucked her breath in. They were prisoners on a pirate ship!

"Matty," Laila said, desperately trying to grab his left hand with her right without success, "Maybe we should go back."

"I know it's frightening, Laila, but nothing bad can happen to us. If we come close to death, we can always wish ourselves back as we always do," Matty told her in the quietest voice he could use and still be heard over the sound of breaking waves.

"We are already. I didn't want to escape to a nightmare. I wanted to go somewhere warm and cozy and have a good time."

"Cozy escapes are nice, but adventures like this can be fun too. Aren't you just a little curious to see what happens next?" Matty asked. Laila could tell he wasn't ready to return yet, and that he wanted her to experience pirate life with him, at least for a little while.

"I don't know, Matty…" Laila said with hesitation. The truth was pretending to be a pirate was one of Laila's favorite childhood pastimes. She used to spend hours in the backyard with a stick pretending to sword fight Captain Hook or jumping off the deck into the ocean to look for sunken treasure. "Are you sure we can't get hurt?"

"I'm sure. I mean, I think I'm sure. You don't still have a sprained ankle, do you?"

"No. I guess there's no harm in staying, then."

"I don't think so."

"What do you think our backstory is?" Laila asked.

"Well, I can't imagine we are anything but good guys. What crime could we have possibly committed? We're our same age, practically children, and we're much too kind, I believe, to be outlaws in any alternate reality," reckoned Matty.

Suddenly, Laila and Matty heard a shout. "Look Captain, the prisoners are awake!"

Dread filled both Laila and Matty, but they tried to hide it.

"Be brave," Matty whispered.

"I am," Laila said.

"I know. I wasn't telling you. I was telling myself."

A man who seemed to appear out of nowhere stood with his hands on his hips facing Matty. He was very intimidating. He was dressed in dirty, but ornate clothing fit for a king. On his head sat a ridiculous powdered wig that did not at all match his brown beard. At his side was a sword in a hilt, but that did not perturb Matty nearly as much as his row of golden teeth.

"Son of the richest tradesman in all of America, how does it feel to have everything taken from you, held captive on old Prit's ship, with your weak sister your only companion," Captain Prit roared. Following his speech, the entire crew cheered in the ugliest way.

When the sound of the applause dwindled, but before Prit had a chance to say anything else Laila spoke out, "I am not weak." Laila considered herself very brave for defending her strength. Matty considered her very foolish.

The whole ship erupted in laughter after they heard what Laila had said. Matty and Laila, on the other hand, turned pale and became very nervous when they realized what she had done.

Captain Prit switched sides so he could face the girl who defied him. Once Laila had a look at the man, she truly regretted her words.

"What's your name, little one?" Captain Prit snarled.

Laila grew speechless. She couldn't remember her name for a second. Then she felt Matty give her hand a squeeze which gave Laila enough confidence to answer the question.

"My name is Laila, sir," she croaked out.

"Laila, what did you say just a minute ago?" the Captain asked squatting down to get on her eye level.

"I said I'm not weak," Laila shouted.

The pirates had a good laugh again while Prit studied Laila's face. She stared down at her lap too afraid to look him in the eyes.

Captain Prit edged closer to her and Laila responded by bringing her knees into her chest.

"Are you afraid?" Captain Prit said quietly enough that only Matty and Laila could hear. Neither of the two answered.

The pirate put two fingers under Laila's chin and pushed just hard enough so her head would be tilted up to face him. "I'm going to repeat myself one more time. Are you afraid, little one?" he whispered.

"No, I am not afraid. Not afraid of you, at least," Laila declared in a voice that felt foreign to her.

A sly smile slid across Captain Prit's face. He stood up and rubbed his beard while thinking.

"I was going to make the boy a member of the Lioness, if he was willing and cooperative, but it seems the girl might serve our interests better. And with such blue eyes, it makes me think she is a special one," Prit spoke to his crew, "It is true what she says. She is strong although not in body in other ways greater than us. Any man who votes we keep her on board say 'aye'."

A chorus of ayes promptly followed. Laila was happy with this outcome and feeling quite proud of herself while Matty felt humiliated.

"Now, what about this one?" the captain smirked pointing down at Matty. "He couldn't even answer my question."

A scary cry of boos came from the crew. Laila's feeling of victory vanished and was replaced by paralyzing fear for her friend.

"We don't need a stuck-up rich boy on board anyway. Those in favor of making the boy walk the plank say, 'aye'."

Much to Matty's dismay, ayes left the lips of every crewman.

"No, please, no," Laila started to cry. "I'll do anything, just don't make Matty walk the plank."

The captain looked at Laila curiously. "Why such love for your brother? Has he really been so very kind to you that he deserved your courage? And shouldn't you be jealous of him? The lazy kid, the apple of your father's eye, waits for his inheritance while you're forced into those-those corsets, starved for beauty, waiting for the chance to please your family with a fine engagement, but that chance never comes."

Hot tears rolled down Laila's face. She didn't want to think about what Captain Prit had said because there was truth in his words, not only in the reality of the escape but in Laila and Matty's world as well.

Laila did love Matty though, so she pushed down her feelings of resentment and said, "I believe in loving people even if they'll never love you properly back."

"That is why girls are idiots," the Captain spat. "I've changed my mind. Since the girl and the boy are both seeming less promising than I hoped, let's have a little fun with them. Shall we?"

The pirates were quiet, but evil grins spread across their faces as they anticipated what the Captain would say next.

"We'll have them fight with wooden swords. Whoever wins will become the second mate. Whoever loses will walk the plank."

Laila and Matty should have wished themselves back to the real world right then, but they were both too preoccupied to think of it.

Captain Prit signaled for his crewmen to untie Matty and Laila, which was an unpleasant experience because the pirates smelled awful and their hands were rough and filthy.

They set them up with swords in the middle of the ship and the pirates formed a circle around them both to watch and as a barrier to keep them from running away.

Matty and Laila tried their best to conceal their panic. Matty didn't know what to do, but Laila was forming a plan.

"On the count of three, I will shoot my pistol up in the air. That will officially start the fight. You each have a sword and nothing more. Fight the best with it you can. Whoever is forced into surrender loses," Captain Prit announced.

Matty and Laila were standing opposite each other. They looked into one another's eyes, but they couldn't figure out what the other was thinking.

"Three," the captain shouted, and a buzz could be heard coming from the pirates.

"Two." This time there was stomping and clapping. Matty felt like he just might pass out.

"One!" The sound of the pistol fired. The screaming of the barbaric sailors made Laila and Matty's ears ring.

For a minute, it felt like time was standing still, but then they each felt a harsh push on their backs. The pirates taunted and jeered at them. They were dying to see a good fight.

Laila picked up her sword and adjusted herself into a battle stance. The sword was heavier than she had expected, and her arms were already feeling sore from carrying it. She wished she had one of the triplets' toy lightsabers. Laila was good at swinging those around. So good Ben believed she was trained by Obi-Wan Kenobi.

Laila nodded at Matty to tell him that it was okay for him to pick up his sword. With shaking hands and knees, he copied Laila's posture. They took a few cautious steps toward each other. Laila knew that Matty didn't want to harm her, but Matty was doubting his trust in Laila. He was starting to feel bad for being such a jerk toward her at school.

"Come on, already," Captain Prit snarled and Laila took a swing. The sound of metal clashing on metal was music to the pirates' ears.

Matty stood his ground, but he didn't make an advance. He glared into Laila's eyes suspiciously. She stroked his sword with hers from another direction. Then, she looked Matty in the eyes, smiled ever-so-slightly so the pirates wouldn't see, winked and mouthed, "Follow my lead."

Slowly, Matty and Laila engaged in some dramatic play-fighting until it got so intense, they were both dripping with sweat. The pirates, Captain Prit included, were having a ball watching the scene because they believed it was a real fight and not pretend.

Suddenly, Laila paused filling each pirate's heart with a sense of suspense. She tilted her head to the right. Matty glanced over in that direction without moving his head. He noticed a weak spot in the barrier of pirate men. Matty held up three fingers and Laila nodded.

They held their swords high and hit them against each other so perfectly one would have thought it was choreographed. Then, they ran side by side pushing the pirates away with the blunt of their sword before they even knew what was happening.

Matty and Laila sprinted as fast as they could. Captain Prit called his men after them angrily, but the teens were too fast.

They reached the end of the ship. "Where do we go now?" Matty demanded desperately. Laila pointed to a net that was connected to the side of the ship and the mast. Quickly, Laila started to climb it.

"Hurry!" Matty cried. He was just behind her. Laila wanted to scream that she was going as fast as she could, but she knew it would have been a waste of breath.

They reached a platform at the top of the mast called a crow's nest. It's the place pirates use as a look-out point. Laila gasped. A pirate with an eye patch was climbing up and he wasn't far away. Matty turned swiftly and cut the ropes that were tied to the crow's nest with forceful swings of his sword, wielding it more like an ax. Once the last rope was out loose the pirate fell onto the ship. First, they heard a shriek and then they heard a thud. Neither Laila nor Matty bothered looking to see his condition.

"Now, we're stuck up here!" Matty exclaimed.

"Not for long someone's going to scramble up here or they'll chop the mast down and we'll be dead. We have to get off this ship entirely."

"Look! There's an island over there. If we can make it to the water, I think we can swim safely over," Matty suggested.

"It's too far to jump!" Laila said as Matty pulled up one of the ropes that were hanging from the crow's nest.

"Here, grab onto me tightly," Matty said. Laila did as she was told and Matty, holding onto both the girl and the rope, launched off the platform. By repeatedly kicking the mast with all of his force and by using their bodies to create momentum, Laila and Matty swung on the rope back and forth like a pendulum while the pirates roared below them.

"This is going to be the last one," Matty said as the rope swung backward. "We'll be far enough to jump into the ocean this time. I'm going to let go and we're going to fall into the water. Start kicking as hard as you can and swimming outward as soon as you feel the ocean. Alright?" Matty instructed.

Laila bit her lip, closed her eyes, and waited for the feeling of falling to come and it did. It was a gut-wrenching feeling, but the adrenaline rush was incredible.

Then, she felt her dress form a bubble as she plummeted into the cool sea. She remembered what Matty had said. Laila started swimming as hard as she could. She didn't bother looking back until she heard Matty's voice. He was about ten yards behind her.

"Laila," he called going up and down with the waves.

"I'm over here!" Laila shouted as loudly as she could. She waved her hands above her head and kicked her legs furiously so he might see her bobbing above the surface.

"I'm coming to you. Stay there," Matty yelled back before swimming as fast as he could toward her.

Laila trod water until Matty reached her and together they swam toward the island insight. Thankfully the current was in their favor and they both had taken swim lessons. Still, it was a far distance for anyone, and they were exhausted by the time they reached the white, sandy beach.

After they crawled far enough onto the island that the tide couldn't reach them, Matty and Laila collapsed face up letting the sun warm their sore bodies while their hearts began to slow down their pace.

"We made it," Laila sighed.

"We did," Matty laughed. Then they both closed their eyes and thought about everything that happened until Matty said, "What now?"

"I guess we go back home and do homework," Laila frowned.

Matty huffed, "I guess you're right. I'll see you later, then."

"Goodbye, Captain Holt," Laila smiled and then began to think about a warm set of clothes and earning an A on her English paper. Matty thought about taking a long nap on the couch with his cats.

Laila rushed out of Matty's house once their escape was over. His father was supposed to get home five minutes ago. Thankfully, he was running late otherwise they might have been found out. Laila had just pulled out of the driveway and was waiting at the intersection right before Matty's house when his father arrived home. It was a close call, but Matty and Laila's secret was safe.

10 FRIENDS

On Tuesday morning, Laila walked into school expecting not to interact with Matty. She had accepted the fact that they would have to live separate lives in public because that's what Matty was set on.

Laila knew that it wasn't about getting caught taking effugium. It was about his reputation. Laila was an outcast. Laila understood that Matty didn't want to associate with her because he was afraid of becoming an outcast too.

But something in Matty changed during the escape to the pirate's ship. Laila had said something that got Matty thinking. She said she believed in loving people even if they'd never love her back.

Matty had never heard anyone say anything like that before. In his mind, love was reciprocal. His mother loved him, so he loved her back. His friends invited him to parties, so he invited them whenever he hosted. Matty worked hard at his job, so he got paid. Love that wasn't mutual was a radical idea to him.

Laila must be an angel, Matty thought. Matty could have gone on ignoring Laila in school and she would have still waited by the phone for his calls, but he decided he wasn't going to take advantage of her love any longer. After all, he needed her more than she needed him although she wanted him more than he wanted her.

The night before school on Tuesday, Matty walked into his mother's room and saw her folding laundry on the floor. Matty sat down next to her and started to match up pairs of socks.

"Thanks for helping me, baby," Matty's mother said.

"Well, thanks for always doing my laundry for me," Matty said, making his mother smile.

"Matty, did you have something you wanted to talk to me about?" Matty's mother asked this after a few minutes of silent folding.

"Uh, yeah, actually," Matty said unsurprised by her intuition, "I guess I was just wondering what you would do if you were kind of-"

"Kind of what?" she asked gently.

"I don't know, I guess maybe if you kind of treated someone the wrong way, what would you do to show them that you loved them and that you made a mistake?" Matty said without making eye contact.

Matty's mother wanted to ask who the question was about, but she also wanted to respect her son's privacy so she gave a rather generic answer, "I think that I would tell them. I would apologize and I'd try to find some way to make it up to that person."

Matty nodded. His mother always gave the best advice.

So, he devised a plan, a plan that would have seemed unthinkable to him a few weeks before. Matty was going to sit with Laila at lunch. It may not seem like much to those who forget what a ruthless society high school social hierarchy creates, but to both Matty and Laila it was a big deal.

On that day, Laila had gotten to the cafeteria early so she sat down at an empty table arbitrarily, expecting some of the other less popular kids to join her. She put in her earbuds, pulled out a book, and started to zone out into her own world while she munched on her Goldfish crackers and sipped her CapriSun. Then, she felt a tap on her shoulder. She turned around in her seat and was shocked to see Matty standing behind her with a big, goofy smile on his face.

She pulled the headphones out of her ears and said rather forwardly, "What are you doing?"

"I was just wondering if that seat next to you was empty," Matty said pointing to the chair on her left.

Laila pulled the chair out to gesture that it was and Matty sat down.

"Listen, I wanted to say that I'm sorry," Matty said.

"For what?" Laila asked.

"For ignoring you in school yesterday and honestly for not being your friend for the last twelve years. I was being stupid, and I realized that, and I guess what I'm trying to say is will you give me a second chance?"

Laila rolled her eyes, "Of course, I will," she groaned sarcastically.

Matty grinned from ear-to-ear and then pulled out a partially crushed carnation from his bag. "I stopped by the florist this morning and got this for you. To say I'm sorry and to tell you that you're a good friend."

Laila lifted the flower up to her nose and smelled it. "It's beautiful," she gushed, "Thanks, Matty." She didn't shove it in her bag as Matty did; she kept it on the lunch table next to her and carried it around with her proudly from class to class for the rest of the day.

Matty pulled out his packed lunch and the two started to eat side by side. Eventually, some unassuming freshmen who knew little about Matty and nothing about Laila sat next to them, but they kept to themselves, of course.

Some people looked and noticed that the homecoming king was sitting with the quirky girl. Some whispered about it with their friends. Some thought it was strange and some girls were jealous of Laila. But nobody said anything. In the end, there wasn't much to say. You're allowed to sit with whoever you want in the cafeteria and eventually people get over it. If they don't, it's not your problem.

Laila always thought she wanted someone to talk to about politics and art and science, but when she was sitting there at the lunch table with Matty she realized that it didn't matter what they talked about as long as it was important to one of them.

So, Matty and Laila talked about all of the normal high school things like the classes that were giving them the most trouble, the new movies coming out, and how their families were sometimes such pains.

"Are you free to stop by again this afternoon?" Matty asked toward the end of the lunch period.

"No, I can't, I have to watch the triplets," Laila explained.

"Oh, that's a shame."

"I know. I'd much rather come over to your house than be stuck with three five-year-olds," Laila complained.

"It can't be that bad, right? I mean they've got to be kind of fun."

"Fun sometimes but a handful. You should meet them sometime."

"I'd like to," Matty said genuinely.

"If you're not doing anything you can come by today. I know the triplets would love to meet a new face and it's always good to have some extra eyes on them."

Matty agreed and Laila gave him her address so he could meet her at her house after school. He had no idea what he was getting into.

"The triplets have morning kindergarten, so they come home all antsy from it," Laila explained to Matty as she ushered him into her smaller but more crowded house.

"Nothing wrong with that," Matty said.

"Here they are," said Laila as they reached the living room. The triplets were busy eating a snack while watching *Spongebob Squarepants* on TV. She pointed to each of her siblings, "That one's Aaron, that's Charlotte, or Lottie, and that's Ben."

"Hello," Matty waved somewhat shyly.

"Laila, who's he?" Ben asked with a mouthful of pretzels.

"My friend, Matty from school. He wanted to play with us today."

"Is he your BOYfriend?" Charlotte asked with wide eyes.

"No, Lottie," Laila answered as calmly as she could despite the embarrassment.

"I didn't know you had friends," Aaron said, not noticing there was anything rude about verbalizing his observation.

"Aaron! That's not very nice," Laila scolded, but Matty just laughed. Laila gave him a mean look.

"What?" Matty chuckled, "You got to admit that was a little funny."

Laila ignored him and sat down on the floor.

"So, Ben," Matty said sitting down on the couch next to him, "What kind of fun things do you like to do?"

Ben gave Matty a strange look. He was still unsure of why this boy was in their house. "I like to build forts," he answered shyly.

Matty gasped, "What a coincidence that is because I have a Ph.D. in fort-making."

Ben squinted at him, "Really?"

"Really."

Ben belly laughed.

"Come on. Show me your pillows and blankets. We'll make the best fort you've ever seen."

Aaron and Charlotte begged to help too, so that's what all five of them did.

They started by dragging all of the comforters and pillows from the bedrooms and closets downstairs. Then, they set up the kitchen chairs strategically around the living room and carefully draped the blankets over top forming a dark cozy den.

At first, they hid out in the fort with flashlights while Laila made up scary stories to tell, not too scary, of course, more or less the stories were goofy tales about haunted toilets and skeleton cats.

The triplets became bored of this after a while, so Matty changed the game to monster, which was basically hide-and-seek tag, but Matty added a twist by pretending to be a Yeti. Even Laila got into the game. She was starting to think this wasn't going to be such a horrible afternoon, after all. The house was a mess and filled with running kids, shrieks, and laughter but that didn't matter to anyone. They were just having a good time.

Eventually, Laila told them it was time to go outside as her mother had recommended. Laila and Matty helped the triplets bundle up and they went out back into the small yard.

Usually, the triplets just fought on the swing set whenever they were forced to play outdoors, but Matty spotted a soccer ball in the corner and got them all involved in a game. The triplets played against the older two. Due to Laila's extreme lack of athletic skills, the triplets won.

Matty was showing off his ball tricks when Mrs. Jennings returned home from the pottery studio. Aaron, Charlotte, and Ben were so mesmerized by Matty when their mother came into the backyard the triplets didn't bombard her for attention as was their norm.

Laila's mother pulled her to the side, "What's going on?" she asked.

Laila knew she was in trouble. She had meant to have Matty leave before her mother got back, but she lost track of time. Her parents had a rule about asking them before having guests over. "I'm sorry," Laila said looking apologetically over at Matty, "I just wanted him to hang out and meet the triplets, so he came over and was helping me watch them."

Matty noticed Mrs. Jennings' disappointment so she smiled at him politely because she didn't want him to think she was rude.

"Mommy," Charlotte cried running over to hug her mother, "Matty helped us build the biggest fort ever."

"Is that so?" Laila's mother grinned.

"Mhmm. And he played monster with us," she added.

"Alright," Mrs. Jennings said, her mood changing, "I'm glad you guys had fun."

"Hi," Matty said, walking over to Laila's mother, "I hope you don't mind that I came over. You have a lovely house."

"No, of course not," Mrs. Jennings lied, "Thanks for entertaining the kids."

"Well," Matty said awkwardly, "I better be on my way. I'll show myself out."

"That's okay. I'll walk you to the door," Laila said.

Matty and Laila walked through the house to the front door while her mother and siblings chatted about their day in the yard.

"Sorry about that," Laila apologized, "Mom doesn't always like when we have people over with her knowing."

"I'm sorry then, too," Matty said, rubbing his forehead.

"It's okay. She'll get over it," Laila chuckled half-heartedly.

"I have to say this was one of the most enjoyable afternoons I've had in a long time," Matty said.

"I'm glad. I had more fun than I expected."

"See ya tomorrow!" Matty waved as he headed to his car.

"See ya tomorrow," Laila waved back.

That afternoon would start a joyous six weeks of what Laila would later think of as the golden days. Laila told her parents what a great guy and friend she thought Matty was and so they let him come over to the house and hang out with the family whenever he wanted. Which was pretty much all the time except for when Matty and Laila needed to go to Matty's house to escape.

They still had to strategically plan when they were going to take the effugium because they couldn't allow anyone to see or find out what they were doing. Essentially, the only place and time they could take effugium was in Matty's bedroom when his parents weren't home and they both had, at least, two hours to spare.

Although the world seemed brighter now that they had each other in it, both Matty and Laila still enjoyed going on their escapes. Sometimes Matty really needed to destress and sometimes Laila really needed the thrill.

They escaped to many different places and times and got to see themselves in many different bodies. Sometimes the escapes were exciting like when they were at a ball of King Louis XIV. Sometimes the escapes were fun like when they went to Coney Island to ride the Cyclone. Sometimes they were peaceful like the escape they had on Valentine's Day.

Laila opened her eyes after taking the effugium. She was sitting on a camping chair looking out on a vast lake. The sun was setting. A cool breeze blew past and refreshed her for a moment as the air was still very warm. Laila listened to the sound of frogs croaking and crickets chirping. She noticed a small island out in the middle of the dark, blue lake. The island was a vibrant shade of green for it was covered in many trees.

Laila looked down and saw her sandalled feet in the sand of the narrow beach. They looked old to her with unfamiliar wrinkles and dark spots. Laila studied her hands and noticed they were the same way. On her right finger, there was a dainty wedding band with a single diamond. It was modest, but Laila admired it very much.

She was wearing light wash jeans and a t-shirt from her future alma mater. Laila felt like she was in her mother's body. It was a strange feeling that made Laila feel proud and comfortable yet scared and discouraged at the same time.

There was a glass of white wine in the cupholder of her camping chair. Laila stared at the glass. She had never had more than a single, quick sip of any alcoholic beverage before. She remembered the taste of her mother's rosé she tried a few years back. Laila had despised it, but because she was "older" now she thought she would try it.

Laila brought the glass to her lips and took a slow, deliberate sip. She held it in her mouth for a moment before swallowing.

"Ugh!" she said scrunching up her face in disgust. It tasted bitter and unusual. Laila poured the remainder of the beverage into the sand and heard a deep chuckle come from beside her.

Laila glanced to her left and smiled. There sat a man who could only, of course, be Matty. He looked very different from any of the Matty's she had seen before.

He had significantly more wrinkles on his brow line and around his eyes. His curly, dark brown hair was starting to gray in spots. There was something about his posture that gave Laila the perception that he was chronically tired.

Matty was dressed in a pair of blue jeans and a Long Beach Island, NJ, t-shirt. Laila could still see a bit of definition in his arm muscles, but he had filled out more. He wasn't overweight but there was a slight roundness to his abdomen.

Laila looked down at Matty's hands. They were aged similarly to hers. She noticed a plain, golden band around his right, ring finger.

Then, it struck Laila that she and Matty were married in this escape. Although they had been a couple in the winter escape it seemed less real and neither of them thought much of it because it wasn't in the timeline of their life. It seemed to Laila and Matty that this escape was.

Unlike in their very first escape, they weren't experiencing a day they had lived with older minds, but a day they had yet to live with younger minds.

Laila looked into Matty's brown eyes. His eyes and his smile were two things that never seemed to change. Laila smiled gently, the way she would whenever she would watch the triplets run around in the sprinkler from the kitchen window.

Matty took a sip of wine from a glass that was identical to Laila's. "It's not that bad," he teased, placing the glass back into his cup holder.

"I don't think I'll ever like the taste of it," Laila declared.

"Never, really?" Matty asked, raising an eyebrow. "I bet you will one day."

Laila shook her head, "It's gross."

Matty laughed. "This is nice," he said staring out at the peaceful landscape.

"Yeah," Laila agreed, watching as a pair of fireflies flew by, "I almost feel like I could stay here forever."

Matty sighed. "Yes, but I think there are good things that come before this."

Laila blushed. "Oh, yeah, of course. I wouldn't wish away our youth."

Matty pulled his shirt up slightly and then turned to Laila with a face of sarcastic shock and horror.

"Laila," he said in a soft voice but with a sense of urgency, "There is *hair* around my belly button."

Laila laughed obnoxiously. She thought it was the most hilarious thing Matty had ever said in an escape.

"Matty Alexander, let me see!" Laila cried enthusiastically in a tone that reminded Matty more of her sister, Charlotte, than her mother.

"No!" he announced quickly before pulling down his shirt in a swift motion.

"How bad is it?" Laila pried with a mischievous grin she just couldn't hide.

"Actually, not that bad," he admitted honestly.

"It's weird being in such an older body," Laila reflected while re-examining herself.

Matty nodded. "It is. I think that is what I will think about when it's time to go back today, my younger body."

"Well, I say we at least try out these old bodies before we make a judgment call. Come on, let's take a walk," Laila said, standing up.

Matty followed Laila and they slowly made their way down the narrow beach. It took a little bit of time to get used to walking in their middle-aged bodies. Balancing on the uneven shore was more difficult than it would have been for them usually. Plus, Laila had a slight, persistent ache in her knees and back.

"I see what they say about growing old," Matty muttered.

"What's that?" Laila inquired.

"It's no fun," Matty giggled.

"Sure, it is," Laila contradicted him, ignoring the fact that she was feeling sore, "This is better than any walk home I endured throughout middle school."

"Middle school doesn't count. Those are everyone's dark years," Matty said in the monotone voice he used whenever delivering deadpan humor.

"I guess I can't argue with you there."

Matty and Laila walked quietly until dusk.

"I have something to say," Matty announced suddenly.

"What is it?"

"I'm scared to grow old."

"Me too," Laila admitted.

"It's the worst thing about being alive, I think. Every day after your twenties, your body starts to deteriorate a little bit and you become less and less yourself. So, you end up spending your best years trying to beat the clock and get everything done that you know you wouldn't be able to later on and that's miserable too."

"What you described is an awful way for anyone to exist," Laila murmured.

"It's the only way," Matty replied.

"It can't be the only way."

"How do you think people should live, Laila," Matty asked. He really did want to know.

Laila pondered the question for a moment. "If people lived in moments, instead of always thinking about the past or the future, ya know. It's cliché, but I think that if people lived in the present for the present things would be better. They'd be happier. Everyone would be happier."

"But what if the present sucks?"

"It does sometimes."

"I guess you'd have to think about the past or the future then."

"I think that's one of the most insightful things you've ever said."

"Maybe."

"It's dark. Let's go explore that cabin," Laila said pointing to a large house up on a hill a few hundred feet away from the lake.

Matty agreed so they went up and looked around the vacation home they assumed could one day be theirs. Of course, neither said so. They didn't want to jinx anything.

Laila and Matty ended up roasting marshmallows and making s'mores on the fire pit by the cabin's patio. They turned on the television inside, but they didn't recognize any of the actors or actresses in the movies. There was nothing inherently special about any of it, but that's what made the whole thing so memorable.

That and the fact it would become their last escape for a very long time.

11 THE DAY OFF

"Matty," Laila waved as she saw him from across the school parking lot. Matty grinned at her greeting. It was 7:30 a.m., and a Monday, but somehow Laila was in a good mood. She was cheery most of the time. In her eyes, the world was beautiful and so she smiled unless there was reason to be sad.

"Good morning, Laila," Matty shouted back. All of the kids smoking in their cars, listening to one last song, or frantically searching for their homework looked at him, but he didn't care. Matty was changing and proud of it.

There were only three months left in Matty's public school career. After graduation, he wouldn't see most of the students from Richardsville High ever again; except for one. he hoped. If the rest of the school thought he was weird, Matty didn't care. It was a small price to pay to show the one person in the world who did matter that he was kind.

"Matty, I have an idea," Laila said as Matty approached her. He could tell from the glimmer in her eye that it was going to be an interesting idea whatever it was.

"What is it, Laila?" Matty asked.

Laila grinned mischievously. "Let's skip."

"Skip? Like, skip into school?"

Laila giggled. "No, tomorrow we can do that. Let's skip school."

"Oh, really?" Are you sure you want to do that? We'll be marked absent and then they'll call out parents." Matty didn't know what his mother and father would think about him skipping school especially to hang out with a girl.

"Yeah, come on. It'll be like Ferris Bueller's day off! You just need to be in bed by the time your parents get home and fake a little cough. Tell them you suddenly weren't feeling good this morning."

"Okay," Matty said with uncertainty. "Well, what will your parents say?"

"My parents were art majors in college. I don't think they'll be able to say anything about me skipping one day of my senior year."

Matty didn't understand what Laila's parents being art majors had to do with anything, but Laila seemed pretty sure of herself so Matty decided to go with it.

"Well," Matty said, scratching his head as the school's warning bell went off. "Where to first?"

Laila shrugged, "That's the fun of it. We get to decide, right here, right now, and then go do it. It's called spontaneity."

"Brilliant. Let's go. We can take my car," Matty cheered. The pair hopped in Matty's small Chevy and drove out of the parking lot. Nobody noticed or suspected a thing because they were too focused on getting themselves to class on time, too tired to care, or too stupid to question anything.

"I'm supposing you'd like to escape," Matty said, turning the familiar corner that would lead to his house.

"Yes, but not with one of those pills," Laila said.

Matty noticed disdain in Laila's voice when she said the word, pills. It was like she had said a dirty word. Matty was confused and a little hurt. He thought that Laila had enjoyed their escapes together.

"What do you mean, then?" Matty asked while driving around the block with no direction.

"Don't get me wrong, Matty. I do enjoy our effugium escapes, but I have something else in mind for today. See, I think we can escape without leaving reality. We can escape in these bodies."

Matty still did not understand because he wasn't as imaginative as Laila.

"So, how are we going to do that?" Matty asked.

"Well, park the car for a second," Laila suggested and so Matty did. He parked in front of somebody's little suburban home with an American flag flying on the porch and a tree with a tire swing.

"Close your eyes," Laila said and they both did. "Now, imagine your life as a movie and you're the star and today is the climax of the movie. Where would you go? What would you do?" Laila asked as the two thought about what the movie would look like and sound like.

"I think that I would go to Disney World," Matty admitted. He couldn't think of anything better. Creativity was not his strong suit.

"Something more realistic, Matty," Laila chuckled.

"Alright, then. I think that I would go wherever you wanted to go because you always have the best ideas."

Laila smiled. Matty's compliment was the most flattering thing she had heard all year. "I would go to the diner and order a triple stack of chocolate chip pancakes and a milkshake and I would sit in a booth, not at the counter," Laila said.

Matty's eyes brightened up. "That sounds absolutely amazing," he said, "but you have to promise not to make fun of me if I order a strawberry milkshake. It's my favorite flavor, but everyone tells me it's girly."

"I promise, but you need to promise me that you are going to stop listening to people who assign gender to flavors."

Matty agreed and drove the two miles to Richardsville Family Diner. It was a bit of a run-down place with a menu that was way too long. The inside still smelled like smoke even though it had been years since smoking was outlawed in Pennsylvania restaurants. The booths were still upholstered with vinyl aquamarine fabric that squeaked when you sat down. When Laila was a little girl, she liked to watch the cakes and pies turn in the revolving glass display case. When Matty was a little boy, he would beg for a chance to play the claw machine game. His parents would give a dollar to Matty and he would try to win one of the world's cheapest-made teddy bears and lose, but Matty was never upset because it was just fun to play.

The hostess gave Matty and Laila a strange look. She considered asking them why they weren't in school, but it didn't really matter to her. The two were seated in the back of the restaurant which was nice because it gave them privacy.

"Matty," Laila asked as the two looked through the menu, "What do you want when you grow up?"

Matty hated questions like these because thinking about the future was not something he enjoyed. "I think I'll try and become a lawyer, maybe. I don't know."

"No, I didn't mean what job do you want to do. I meant what do you want for yourself."

Matty shook his head. No one had asked him that before. "I don't know. What do you want?"

Laila had been thinking of what she wanted for a long time. "There's a lot of things I might want, things that would be nice to have, but I guess there is only one thing I really want and that would, of course, be to be happy."

Matty nodded, "Yeah, I guess that's all really anyone can hope for."

"To expect anything else in addition to happiness would just be ungrateful," Laila added very seriously.

"So, what do you need to be happy?" Matty probed. He hoped her answer might give him insight into his own life.

"I think I need someone who I can talk to and I think I need a cozy place to read books."

"That's it? No wedding ring. No elegant house. No career aspirations you're dying to accomplish?"

Laila thought for a moment. It would be nice to have those things, but she knew she could be happy without them.

"Well, I guess it might be nice to get married, but only if I found the right person. I would never want to marry just to marry. If I found someone I could talk to and we were in love, then I suppose I would want to marry them. An elegant house wouldn't suit me at all. I'm the opposite of elegant. I don't know exactly what I want my career to be. I think I could do a lot of different things, but I don't think that I could do one thing for my entire life. That would be so boring. I just want to help people and create things and go places."

Matty liked her answer. It was exactly what he hoped she would say. "I agree about the house and the career, but I do want to get married," Matty said.

"Why's that?" Laila asked as politely as she could.

"Because it's the right thing to do when you love someone," Matty answered matter-of-factly.

The waitress came and took their orders. Matty ordered a strawberry milkshake and Belgian waffles with strawberries and whipped cream. Laila ordered chocolate chip pancakes with a chocolate milkshake.

While they ate, they played twenty questions. Matty found out that Laila's favorite flower was a water lily, her favorite color was yellow, and her favorite song was *Penny Lane* by The Beatles. Laila learned that Matty liked tulips because those were his mother's favorite, the color blue, and the song *Delicate* by Taylor Swift. Laila had to vow again that she wouldn't tell anyone that Matty liked Swift's music. Admitting to that as a high school boy would have been social suicide.

Out of the blue, Laila asked Matty what Disney princess he would be.

"What kind of question is that Laila? He replied with a raised eyebrow.

"I don't know. Just answer it."

"Well, why can't I be a prince?"

"Because the princes are boring and one-dimensional. Stop trying to avoid the question. I'm not going to think you're any less masculine for answering it," Laila rebutted.

"Well, I guess I'd be Cinderella. She works hard, right?"

"Right, that's a good answer, then."

"Now, it's your turn. Who would you be?"

"That's easy. I'd be Belle. She's smart and she loves to read, and she doesn't fit in," Laila explained.

"I'm starting to think that not fitting in might not be so bad," Matty admitted.

Laila smiled gently, "I've never really fit in. And it's nice when you stop worrying about trying to fit in because you can just be you, but it's lonely sometimes, Matty. Sometimes I wonder if it's better to be me and be lonely or maybe it would be better if I tried to be a little bit more normal because the loneliness really hurts sometimes."

Matty felt angry. Laila was one of his favorite people in the world. She didn't deserve to feel lonely and she didn't deserve to feel like she wasn't normal.

"Laila, did you know that even people who do fit in can feel lonely? Do you remember the day that I was crowned homecoming king?" Matty asked.

"I think so…" Laila said.

"That day I was so lonely. I felt like there was no one I could talk to. I had a panic attack the morning before school that day. I don't know why. Nothing seemed to trigger it. It just happened. And so, for the rest of the school day, I wanted to just go home and be alone, but I couldn't. I had to pretend like I was having the greatest day of my life. I didn't have anyone to tell how anxious and depressed I was feeling that month. You see, the day I won the school's biggest popularity contest was one of the loneliest days of my life." Matty looked down at his plate and felt sorry for himself and for Laila.

"I know," Laila said after a moment.

"What do you mean?"

"I know that you were sad. Not only on that day but others too. I could see it in your eyes. You would smile with the rest of your face, but your eyes would never lie. That's how I knew," Laila explained.

Matty smiled. It felt good to know that there was someone who understood how he was feeling all that time even if he hadn't known it.

"What am I feeling now?" he asked.

"You're happy," Laila replied, and she was right.

After they were done eating, Matty and Laila left a massive tip, well massive for two teenagers, because they were happy and feeling generous.

"That was one of the best breakfasts I've ever had," Laila said as they got back into Matty's car. Matty said it was the best he had ever had in his entire life which made Laila's heart beat a little faster.

Laila told Matty she wanted to show him something at the park and so that's where they went next. It was only nine in the morning and the air was chilly. The sun was bright like it is at the end of March. Laila noted the smell of springtime in the air.

When Matty and Laila arrived, there were few people in the park, an elderly couple walking their pug and a college-aged girl going for a jog.

"So, what did you want to show me?" Matty asked as he looked around the park. He had been there before for Easter egg hunts, soccer games, and Independence Day picnics when he was younger, but it had now been years since he had been in the park. That is with the exception of Matty and Laila's first escape together. Matty thought to himself that he should remember to come down to the park more often because it was a nice place to be, kind of like the woods, but less lonely.

"My favorite spots," Laila said, "First, are the swings because I've always been really good at swinging high and it's a lot of fun because as you try to swing higher and higher the more you feel like you're flying. And when you feel like you're flying you feel like you're invincible and nothing can hurt you."

"I think I would like that," Matty said. The boy and the girl hopped on a pair of swings and they each began to swing as high as they could. Matty was not able to swing as high as Laila, but they both were under the illusion they were reaching the 'top'.

"Do you feel invincible yet, Matty?" Laila shouted when she heard him laugh from joy.

"Yeah, I think so. Do you?" he shouted back.

"Yeah, I do. Now, when you reach the highest point, in that second before you swing backward, make a wish."

"What kind of wish?" Matty yelled.

"The kind you make when you blow out candles on a birthday cake."

"Alright, then. I wish that I could feel invincible forever."

Laila let out a roar of laughter, the free kind of laughter that sometimes makes others stare and wish they had the same kind of glee. Laila hadn't meant for them to say their wishes out loud. She had always kept hers in her mind before, but she liked the way Matty had done it and so she decided to try it too.

When Laila reached the top she hollered, "I wish that Matty Alexander Holt would be happy for the rest of his life."

Matty's heart soared when he heard Laila's wish. For a second, he believed it would come true. The two continued to take turns shouting wishes.

"I wish that Laila Willow Jennings will live to be 101!"

"I wish that Matty will live as long as I do."

"I wish that we could feel this young forever."

"I wish that no one would ever get hurt again."

"I wish that I would become the richest man alive."

"I wish that the triplets would all become millionaires."

"I wish that my grandchildren will come and visit me when I'm old."

"I wish that I'll be the fun aunt."

'I wish that college will be easy."

"I wish that college will be fun."

"I wish that Laila would go to a Taylor Swift concert with me."

"I wish that Matty wouldn't ever feel lonely again."

"I wish that Laila would never change to fit in."

"I wish that we could be done making wishes," Laila finally said. Both were getting dizzy from swinging so high for so long.

They let the swings stop and sat quietly for a moment letting the dizziness fade away while they held onto the memory of the wish-making so that it could stay with them forever.

"That was fun," Matty mumbled almost to himself.

"I hoped you would say that," Laila said. "I think you'll like my next favorite spot too."

Matty followed Laila to the oak tree they had climbed together in their first escape. He watched as Laila pushed herself up onto the lowest branch. Laila glanced down at Matty who had a sort of strange expression on his face. It was like happiness, sadness, confusion, and pride all in one.

"Aren't you going to join me?" Laila asked teasingly.

Matty snapped out of his feelings. "Oh yeah, but we'll look a little odder, now won't we?" Matty said as he began to climb.

"We were just shouting out wishes on the swings. It can't look sillier than that."

Matty nodded and they climbed up to the branch they had sat on before in their escape.

Laila looked around when she reached the top. She thought it was funny how some things changed, and some things hadn't. The slides and the swings and the merry-go-round were in the same spots waiting for children to come to play on them as they had been ten years ago, but the red and blue paint that had made them so cheerful was chipping. Rust was starting to form around the bolts.

Everything seemed a bit smaller too. This time not because they were viewing it from a higher position, but because they had grown and seen more of the world. Laila admired the creek though because as far as she could tell it had not changed. It still ran through the same part of the park and at the same pace it always had. It still made the same peaceful bubbling noises and was still home to little minnows and ducks as it had been for as long as Laila and Matty could remember.

Matty and Laila had talked a lot that day already. Although they hadn't run out of things to say, they both needed a break from moving their mouths and so they sat and just enjoyed being. Matty and Laila just were, and it was enough for them. Then, Matty pulled out his phone and a set of earbuds.

"Let's listen to our favorite songs together," he suggested.

"Okay, show me your favorite sad song first," Laila said and Matty pulled up *Sign of the Times* by Harry Styles. Laila hadn't heard it before. She wasn't against pop music or pop stars, but she didn't expose herself to it either. She cried not because it was such a sad song, but because she knew how it made Matty feel.

"Why are you crying?" Matty asked because he hadn't seen Laila cry before.

"Because I can see you. I can see you listening to this song and being sad that you were born into this time and it makes me sad because I don't want you to feel that way, Matty," Laila explained.

Matty wiped away the tears that were on Laila's cheeks. "It's okay," was all that he could say because Laila was right. He did listen to the song when he was feeling that way, but he wanted to push those thoughts out of his head because this was supposed to be a happy day.

"Show me your favorite sad song," he said, handing her his phone.

Laila pulled up *Eleanor Rigby* by The Beatles, of course. Matty didn't cry. He smiled which confused Laila.

"Why are you smiling at my sad song?" she asked.

"Because we used to be like all the lonely people and now, we're not, right?" Matty grinned.

Laila had to think about it for a second before she realized it was true then she brightened up. "Right," she said handing the phone back to Matty, "Now show me your favorite music video."

Matty and Laila watched the music video for *Take On Me* by A-Ha. Laila figured out pretty quickly why Matty liked it. Laila chose *Shake It Off* by Taylor Swift to humor Matty. He got a kick out of it. It wasn't Laila's favorite music video. She didn't make a point of watching them, so she thought she would use the opportunity to make Matty laugh.

"I do like the way they dance in this," Laila admitted. "I kind of like to dance like that in front of the mirror when I'm bored at home in my bedroom."

Matty scrunched up his nose. "Really?" he asked skeptically. He couldn't picture it.

"Really. Honest," Laila swore, placing her hands on her heart.

"I'll believe it when I see it," Matty winked. He did believe her, but it was fun to tease.

Laila and Matty spent the next hour listening to songs through one earbud together until Laila remembered she still had one more favorite spot to show Matty.

"I think you're going to like this spot the best," Laila said as they hobbled down the tree.

Laila brought Matty to the place she liked to go when the triplets were driving her up the wall and she needed a breather. It was a small wooden bench in the flower garden, except this time of year there weren't any flowers growing and the small fountain was empty.

"It's not so nice until April," Laila admitted blushing because she felt stupid for bringing Matty there. It didn't feel as special to her as it had before. Laila thought maybe it was just a better place for being alone.

"It's just a bench until you tell me why it's special," Matty implored.

"I do my best thinking and reading and writing here sometimes," Laila said, feeling a little self-conscious for reasons she couldn't understand.

"Have you ever written anything about me, here?" Matty blurted out. He regretted it though shortly after. He knew it was impolite to ask, but he wanted to know. He thought that if he were a writer like Laila that he would write about her.

Laila smirked. "No," she lied.

"Well, I think you should," Matty said cockily.

"Why's that?" Laila asked.

"I'm complex. I'm messed up and I'm on some crazy meds. Is that enough?"

"Whatever," Laila rolled her eyes. She didn't want to let on that she already was writing about him because writers write about what's on their hearts. Laila had no choice but to tell Matty's story.

"I'm hungry," Matty said suddenly.

"Already?" Laila asked. She hardly ate as much as Matty did and she felt like they had just had breakfast.

"Come on, let's go to my house. We can make sandwiches," Matty proposed.

"Do you know how to make anything else?"

"No," Matty answered unashamedly as they walked toward his car.

"Good. Sandwiches are my favorite," Laila declared. She was a bad cook herself.

So, they went to Matty's house and had a wonderful afternoon. First, they ate peanut butter and fluff sandwiches with cream soda and cheese curls because Matty said they hadn't eaten enough sweet food yet on their day off.

Later, they jumped in Matty's pool because Laila said it was something that would happen if their lives were movies.

"Ready, Matty?" Laila asked as she stood on the edge looking into the inground pool Matty had just uncovered.

"Do we have to do this?" Matty asked, rolling his eyes. It seemed stupid to him.

"Yes," Laila insisted. She didn't want to do it anymore. The pool didn't look inviting and a cool breeze had just blown past and chilled her more.

"Alright, then. It's going to be cold though," he warned.

"Count down. 1...2...3..." Splash. Laila cannonballed in the pool and Matty followed right after. He wanted to see if she was going to go through with it first. He didn't want to be tricked.

"Ahhh!" Laila shrieked as she swam to the ladder. She was out in a second, but Matty stayed in. He wanted to see how long he could last in the freezing water.

"It was your idea," he reminded Laila as she stood shaking.

"It was dumb. Nobody's filming us."

"I know. Now you have to wait. I think I might want to stay in a little longer," Matty teased before diving down below the water.

"Can we go inside, please? I'm really cold, Matty," Laila begged when Matty's head came above water.

"Yeah, let's go. We're never doing that again," Matty declared as he climbed out of the pool shivering when the cold air hit him.

Matty and Laila dripped water all over the kitchen until they reached a linen closet where Mrs. Holt kept her best fluffy, white towels. Matty grabbed two and tossed one to Laila.

"I can give you some of my Mom's clothes," Matty offered.

"Are you sure she won't mind? I could probably just wear some of yours..." Laila asked nervously. She didn't know Mrs. Holt very well. Laila thought she would feel kind of weird wearing her clothes.

"Yeah, it's fine. I'll just let you wear some of the stuff she never does. She'll never notice. Then, you can give it back to me later. I'll wash them, put them back, and she'll never even know."

Laila hesitated. Laila was a girl so she knew that Matty didn't understand how women care for their clothes, but she was also dying to get out of her wet jeans so she agreed.

Laila waited in the hallway as Matty rummaged through his mother's stuff until he came out with a pile of clothes he thought would fit. Laila took them into the bathroom gratefully as Matty went to his room to change.

The clothes were a little too big, but Matty's mother was petite as well so it wasn't too bad. Laila felt much more comfortable in the sweats and sweatshirt than she had before, so she was glad. Laila put her wet clothing into a grocery bag Matty had given her and walked nervously to his bedroom door and waited. She didn't want to disturb him while he was changing.

Eventually, he opened the door. "Pyjamas?" Laila giggled as she watched the water drip from his hair.

"I'm sick, remember?" Matty joked sarcastically.

Laila laughed, "Do you have a hairbrush I could use?" she asked, feeling embarrassed. It felt like a girly thing and it was weird for Laila to talk about girly things not only with boys but with girls as well.

"Oh, yeah," he said nonchalantly as Laila followed Matty into his room which, of course, she was familiar with. Matty pointed to a hairbrush on his dresser. Laila began to comb her hair with it while looking in the mirror. Matty got into his bed but before he laid his head down on the pillow he noticed something about Laila he hadn't before. As he watched her comb through her wet knotted hair, in clothes that were too large, and with no makeup on her face, Matty realized that she was beautiful.

Laila was the most beautiful person on the planet. Matty had never seen it before, but suddenly it was the truest thing he had ever known.

"Laila," he said quietly looking up at the ceiling.

"Mhmm," Laila hummed to indicate that she was listening.

"There's something you need to know."

"What?" she asked, laying the brush down on the dresser as she turned to face Matty.

"You are so beautiful, Laila," Matty said sitting up to look her in the eyes.

Laila blushed, but she didn't feel embarrassed as she had a minute before. She felt something else. She wasn't sure what it was yet. "You think I'm beautiful?" she asked in a small voice.

"Yeah, but it doesn't matter what I think. You are beautiful whether I think it or not. Whether I tell you it or someone else does or no one does, Laila Willow Jennings was, is, and will always be beautiful. And I hope she never forgets it," Matty spoke his mind with vulnerability and it made him feel strong like nothing else had before.

"Matty," Laila said as she climbed into the bed next to him. "That's the nicest thing you've ever said to me and I promise I won't forget it."

Matty smiled. That's all he wanted for some reason now, that Laila would know that.

"Can I tell you something now?" Laila asked, reaching out to hold Matty's hands in her own.

Matty nodded. "I love you and I hope that's enough for you to be happy," Laila whispered.

Laila hadn't expected to say those words. She hadn't thought about saying them out loud before, but she didn't like to hide the truth, so she let out the truth she was feeling at the moment. Matty had never heard someone outside of his family say that they loved him and believed it, but this time he did.

"It's enough," Matty whispered back. It was all he could manage to say at the time.

Matty wrapped his arms around Laila and Laila wrapped his arms around Matty. It was more than friendly, but it wasn't romantic. It was just nice.

It may be difficult for some people to understand, but even though Matty thought Laila was beautiful and she loved him, it didn't cross either of their minds to kiss or do anything more. They didn't even want to date. They both had too much to work out, but in that hug, there was an understanding between the two of them. Laila had found her somebody to talk to and Matty had found his first real friend. Laila knew Matty and Matty knew Laila. That was enough for them, then.

"I'm tired," Matty said as he released Laila from the hug.

"Me too," Laila yawned as if she just then realized she was extremely exhausted.

"Can we take a nap?" Matty asked hopefully.

"Oh, yeah," Laila said looking at the clock. "There's about two hours before either of your parents gets home."

"We can sleep a little bit. Whoever wakes up first can wake the other up. Then, I'll drive you back to your house and be back in bed with a terrible sore throat by the time my mom pulls in," Matty figured.

"Sure," Laila agreed, stepping out of Matty's bed.

"Where are you going?"

"The guest room-"

"Oh,"

"What? Did you think I was going to sleep with you?"

Matty shrugged. "You could. I wouldn't. I mean I'm not ready for *that,* but I do sometimes wish I could wake up with someone next to me."

Laila took a deep breath in. She trusted Matty, but part of her still felt like it was wrong to sleep in a bed with a boy even if he promised not to do anything and she believed him. Then, she remembered all the times she had laid down next to Matty on that bed without the sheets over them as they escaped into other worlds. Would it be that different if they went under the sheets this one time?

"You don't have to, really," Matty said, noticing her uncertainty, "I don't want you to do anything you don't want to do."

"Okay," she said as she got into bed next to Matty, "I do really want to though."

Matty smiled and turned his body to face the opposite direction of Laila. "Goodnight," he murmured before drifting off.

"Goodnight," Laila sighed.

12 CAUGHT

Matty and Laila thought for sure they would wake up before Matty's parents got home. They were seventeen and eighteen and feeling very carefree that afternoon, so neither of them bothered to set an alarm. They trusted their bodies, but that was a mistake.

When Matty's father came home at four in the afternoon, he walked up to Matty's bedroom to say hello and to ask his son about his day. This had become a sort of ritual between Matty and his father since Matty's mental health struggles began. It was Mr. Holt's way of showing that he cared.

When Mr. Holt knocked and didn't get a response, he opened the door a crack and called his son's name softly. Again, he didn't hear anything back, so he decided to just walk in. He was expecting to see his son with headphones on or perhaps not in the room at all. What he was not expecting to see was Matty asleep with his arms wrapped around Laila.

"What the hell is going on here?" Mr. Holt demanded with his hands on his hips.

Laila's eyes popped and she scrambled quickly out of the bed. Matty sat up straight and tried to think of something to say, but his shock left him speechless.

"What are you doing in my wife's clothes?" Matty's father added when he saw what Laila was wearing.

"It's not what it looks like," Matty insisted.

"If it's not what it looks like, then what is it?" Mr. Holt countered.

"Please, don't get mad at Matty. It was all my idea. He didn't want to skip school," Laila interjected.

"You skipped school?" His dad yelled, turning to glare at Matty.

Matty looked down at his hands. "Dad, do we have to do this now?"

"I think it might be best if you went home, now," his father told Laila.

"Yes, sir. I'm sorry," Laila muttered before showing herself out.

Laila took a deep breath and prepared herself for the short drive home.

It had been the most perfect day, but now it had the worst ending. Laila remembered the look on Mr. Holt's face when he discovered them in Matty's bed together. It was easy to assume Matty's father thought they were having sex, but they weren't and that was the worst part. Laila felt terrible for revealing that they had skipped school too. Now, her best friend was in trouble and she probably would be too.

Laila parked the car in her parents' driveway and instantly started to cry. She blamed herself for everything. Laila felt stupid and helpless. She would have done anything at that moment to go back in time and just go to school instead of playing hooky. Normally, she tried to live without regrets, to keep the past in the past, but she couldn't this time.

Laila bit her lip, turned the keys in the ignition, and put the car in reverse. She couldn't go into the house because her parents would see her with her red eyes and puffy face. They would ask her why she was upset, and she wouldn't know what to say.

Laila drove down to the street to the only place she felt like she could go, her grandmother's house. Bravely, Laila walked up the path to the yellow-painted home and she rang the doorbell.

"Laila? I wasn't expecting you. Come on in, darling," Grandma smiled sweetly when she opened the door to find her distressed granddaughter waiting for her anxiously.

"I'm sorry for not calling first," Laila sniffled.

"Oh, don't worry about that, my little fairy. Let's go sit down in the living room. I'll make us some tea and we can chat. It looks like you've had a rough day."

Laila sighed. "That sounds perfect."

Laila's grandmother went to the kitchen and put a kettle of water on the stove while Laila waited in her living room and worked on a puzzle Grandma was in the middle of.

"So," Laila's grandmother said handing her a steaming cup of chamomile tea, "I called your mother and I told her that you and I are going to have a special girls night tonight, just the two of us."

"Thanks, Grandma," Laila smiled, taking a sip of her tea. She was already feeling more relaxed just like she knew she would.

"You're welcome. If you want to talk, we can, or we don't have to. I don't want to be nosy. I'm just glad to have some extra time to spend with you."

Laila inhaled and then exhaled slowly. "I really messed something up. That's all."

"Ah… I see. You know we all mess things up from time to time. But we bounce back, and you will, Laila. Whatever you messed up you'll fix, or it'll fix itself."

Laila felt herself start to choke up. "Are you sure, Grandma?" Laila asked because she wanted to hear her reassuring words again.

"I'm sure," Grandma promised.

"Well, what if I messed things up for someone else?"

"Who is this someone else?"

Laila squirmed a little in her chair. "If I tell you, please don't tell anyone else, okay?"

"Who would I tell?" Grandma laughed.

Laila chuckled a little too. "It's this boy, Matty. And we're not dating or anything, but he's my best friend."

"That makes sense. Best friends are so much more important than sweethearts."

Laila blushed, "Yeah, I guess so. The thing is I don't think he's mad at me. I'm just mad at myself for the situation I put him in."

"Well, that's relieving to hear."

"Why?"

"Because it's a sign of a strong woman."

"To be mad at herself?"

"No, not that in itself. That you care more about how your actions affect others, but that you can also think and feel for yourself."

Laila didn't understand what her grandmother was saying, not yet, but she took it as a compliment anyway. "Thanks, Grandma. You know I've always kind of felt that I was strong."

"And you should!"

Laila sat with her thoughts for a moment while her grandmother sipped her chamomile tea and remembered what it felt like to be seventeen.

"Do you know what I think?" Grandma said after a while.

"What?" Laila smiled, snapping out of her thoughts.

"We should order in."

Laila agreed enthusiastically and the pair enjoyed an evening of story-telling, Scrabble-playing, and eating of Italian food.

When Laila stepped into the cold air that night after saying goodbye to her grandmother and thanking her for a good time she had just as much uncertainty as she had entered with. But as she watched her breath in the darkness, she realized that she could still have peace even with uncertainty.

Somehow, she managed to love her grandmother even a little bit more as well.

13 DROWNING

Matty's parents were pissed. They labeled Laila as a bad influence and believed she was the reason for Matty's cheating and skipping school, although she had nothing to do with the prior.

"Listen, Matty," his mother said, "We just want the best for you and Laila, we don't think she's the best for you right now."

"Mom, please," Matty cried, "You have to understand we didn't do anything. I promise. You have to believe I'm telling the truth."

"So, you're saying you didn't skip school?" Matty's father asked sarcastically.

"No but come on it's my senior year. Kids do it all the time," Matty protested.

"I don't care if other kids do it all the time. I care about what you do and your future," his father countered.

Matty rolled his eyes.

"Baby," Matty's mom said in her good cop voice, "Can you trust me on this one? All we're asking is that you stop spending so much of your time with Laila until the summer, alright."

"Well, what I'm asking is that you don't meet up with her outside of school until the summer. You need to focus on getting yourself back on track, Matty Alexander," Matty's father said in his bad cop voice.

"But she makes me happy…"

"Matty, you don't need a girl in your life right now to make you happy, okay? You need to reset and reconnect with your other friends and then in the fall you'll go to college and make new friends. I know it seems like Laila is everything now, but in a few years, she'll be nothing more than a passing thought when you drive through town," Mr. Holt insisted.

"You're wrong about that," Matty muttered looking away from his parents.

"Matty, we might be wrong. Sometimes even parents make mistakes, but while you're still living in our house please respect us and try to follow our rules. Haven't we always tried our best to take care of you?" Matty's mother was almost on the verge of tears herself as she said this.

Matty stood up from the kitchen table, "Fine. That's what I'll say because I don't have a choice." Then, he walked up to his bedroom.

He cried into his pillowcase and it didn't matter to him whether it was manly or not because he knew stuff like that didn't matter to Laila. Then, his father told him to stop being so dramatic; he had only known the girl for a few months.

Matty decided to write a letter to Laila explaining how cruel he thought his parents were being. He spent hours writing it, or at least that's what it felt like to him. He wrote all these emotional, wonderful, clichés to her. He told her wished he would have said, "I love you," back.

When he was finally done, he read it over and thought it was the best thing he had ever written. Then, he ripped it up and threw it into his wastebasket. What was the point of telling Laila he loved her if he could never see her again?

Instead, he picked up his phone and called Laila. He had gotten all of his feelings out and he was feeling calm now.

"Matty!" Laila exclaimed. It was late at night and she had just gotten home from her grandmother's house.

"Hey, Laila, I have something to tell you-" Matty started.

"Me too. I'm so sorry for everything, Matty. Skipping school was such a stupid thing to do."

"It's alright. I just think we need to take a break," Matty said nonchalantly. He didn't tell Laila that his parents had banned him from seeing her because he didn't like admitting that someone else could control him.

"What?" Laila hoped she had heard him wrong.

"Let's just focus on school and ourselves at least until the summertime."

"I don't understand."

"What's not to understand."

"You don't make any sense, Matty."

"I'm sorry. It's not about you. It's about me. Don't take it so personally."

"So, we're not together, but you're breaking up with me?"

Matty chuckled. "I mean you said it not me."

"Matty, are you being serious? Because I'm not going back and forth with you. If you're going to be like this then there's no more escaping. There's no more hanging out at my house. There's no more eating with me at lunch. So, you better be sure. I'm not playing games with you. I'm worth more than that."

"Yeah, Laila. I'm sure." Matty said quietly.

"Alright, then. Goodbye, Matty," Laila said before hanging up the phone.

Matty took a shower and tried to think of nothing. Now, it was Laila's turn to cry into her pillowcase until she fell asleep.

This became a habit for Laila. She went to school, talked to no one, ate with no one, and counted the days until graduation. Then, she went home, did her homework, spent hours watching trashy reality TV, and cried herself to sleep. And that pattern repeated itself over and over.

Laila wanted to be her optimistic, carefree self again, but she couldn't. She tried so hard. She listened to *Here Comes the Sun* every morning, but the sun never came. She spent time with the triplets, but even they couldn't bring Laila a smile that lasted. She wondered if this was just going to be how life was like for her forever. Grandma told her things would fix themselves, but they weren't.

Matty went back to sitting at the popular table. He went back to smiling while feeling empty inside. Lots of people were happy the old Matty was back. Matty told himself he didn't care either way. He was existing to please others to boost his ego and because he wasn't brave enough to exist for himself yet.

He continued to take the effugium, but he couldn't escape anymore. Now it was just like any other antidepressant or antianxiety medication he had been on. It helped alleviate his symptoms. He was able to function, but deep in his heart he missed Laila and so he was always left with this vague feeling that something was wrong. Matty knew somehow things could never be the same between them, the reason being his pride, but he convinced himself the whole situation was out of his control and there was nothing he could do about it.

From mid-March until their graduation, Matty and Laila lived in a period that Laila would later think of as the "dark ages".

14 CHILDHOOD'S FINALE

Matty and Laila hadn't spoken for months. They hadn't
texted, hadn't waved, and hadn't smiled at each other. Laila tried
not to even look at Matty in school.

Laila still sometimes longed to take effugium and to escape
into a place far away from where the world seemed so grey, but
she couldn't because she wasn't friends with Matty anymore.
Matty still sometimes longed to escape as well, but the medication
didn't work that way for him anymore for some strange reason he
couldn't understand.

Neither Laila nor Matty were able to live in the present.
Laila spent her time thinking about how much better the future
would be for her when she was finally able to go out into the world
and find her own people. Matty was stuck in the past thinking
about the good times he had with Laila and how he would never be
able to have those good times again.

Sometimes Matty wondered if completely cutting out Laila
without giving her a proper explanation of his parents' role was the
right decision. Most times he thought that it wasn't, but he was too
busy feeling sorry for himself to figure out a way to heal the
situation between himself, his parents, and Laila. It was much
easier to keep his feelings bottled up than to risk loving again.

The night of their high school graduation finally came after
what Laila felt like was the longest two and a half months of her
life. Matty was indifferent to the occasion, but Laila was ready in a
bitter sort of way she never imagined she would be like.

Laila wore white and Matty wore red. They received their diplomas, got pictures taken with their family, and said goodbye or good riddance to the school that had been almost their entire world for the past four years. And that's how it ended. After a long time of waiting it felt abrupt and Matty and Laila were both missing closure from the most significant relationship, they had had during high school.

Matty and Laila were feeling sad, but they told themselves it didn't matter. Things were going to get better if only they didn't think. High school was over and so were they.

But their big plans to forget each other fell through.

There was a party after graduation at the school. To keep kids out of trouble they offered them gift cards, chances to win laptops, and free food and then they locked them in the cafeteria. There was dancing, games, and even a hypnotist but no one cared about that because they had just graduated.

Laila didn't want to go, but her mother told her she should in a tone that didn't allow much debate. Matty went because that's what the other kids expected him to do.

Both Matty and Laila pulled up to the school in the dark and parked in the back. They were both running late.

When Laila opened her car door hurriedly, she found herself looking right at Matty who had just gotten out of his car. They made eye contact, but not on purpose.

Laila had a choice. She could flat-out ignore him or she could say hi and be polite because this was the last day of high school, the last day of life as they knew it.

"Hi, Matty," she said quietly and awkwardly.

Matty was surprised that she had greeted him, but he was happy about it because he had missed her.

"Oh, hi, Laila," he replied and the two started to walk toward the building keeping a safe distance between each other.

"This is going to blow," Laila said casually.

"You're right about that," Matty chuckled uncomfortably.

"Congratulations, by the way," Laila said after a moment of silence.

"Oh yeah, you too," Matty smiled.

"You know, I just have to say this, because maybe we won't ever talk again, escaping with you was one of the craziest, most unbelievable, most real things I've ever done. So, thank you for that," Laila spoke in a very low voice so that in case anyone was around they wouldn't be able to hear her.

"I think that we should not go in," Matty said.

"I agree... and if we don't, I'll stay with you. I mean, if that's what you want," Laila told him.

Matty turned and looked into Laila's blue eyes for the first time that night. "What are we waiting for, then?"

Laila's heart raced and she felt all fuzzy inside. Matty's dreamy, trustworthy brown eyes were tricking her again to fall for him. She had hoped for and feared a moment like this. Matty was bad news. He gave her magic and then took it away. Laila remembered how it hurt, how it still hurt. But she wanted Matty and his magic. It was irresistible. He was irresistible.

They walked to his car and he opened the door for her. Matty drove away and Laila stayed quiet. Everything felt eerily familiar.

"Apologies and explanations and fighting back and forth will take too long so can we just pretend that nothing ever happened and we're friends just like we used to be?" Matty asked hopefully.

"We can pretend, but we'll know it's not true, and no matter how well we act it won't be true. As long as you can remember that I'm down."

"It's a deal."

Matty drove up the mountain to the look-out point and he parked his car in the spot that people knew was for cheap romance.

"There's some effugium in there," Matty said pointing to the glove compartment.

Laila opened it and pulled out a plastic sandwich bag with a bunch of white pills inside. She handed it over to Matty.

"I put it in there in case I ever decided to run away," he said as he opened the bag taking four pills out.

"Matty, I say this because I still care for you. Please, please get your mind right this summer," she said while looking straight ahead. Matty put two of the pills into his pocket.

Matty handed the bag back to Laila and she put it back into the glove compartment. Matty didn't say anything.

"Promise," Laila demanded.

"Sure," Matty said half-heartedly. "Here, let's try this again," Matty suggested placing one pill into Laila's palm and one into his mouth.

"Yeah, I 've been wanting to do this for so long," Laila revealed before swallowing the pill. Matty just hoped it would work. After he saw Laila close her eyes, he popped the two other pills he had been hiding into his mouth and entered the escape.

Laila opened her eyes. In front of her was possibly the most alarming thing she had ever seen in an escape. It was a baby and a crying baby.

Matty was standing next to her. "What do we do with it?" he asked, clearly frazzled.

Laila reached into the crib and cradled the baby in her arms. "I guess we just try to comfort her," she said while rocking the little girl back and forth.

Matty looked over Laila's shoulder and into the baby's eyes. Matty and Laila were older, somewhere around the same age they had been in the second escape. They were in pyjamas and standing in a modern-looking nursery. Neither Matty nor Laila knew exactly what to make of the situation.

"Whoever she is, she's adorable," Matty whispered. The baby had stopped crying and was slowly being lulled into sleep.

"I think- I think she might be ours," Laila stuttered.

"Wait, really?" Matty exclaimed the shock evident in his voice.

"I think so. Look she has your nose," Laila pointed.

Matty's head was spinning. He couldn't process what he was seeing. "And your hair and your eyes," he added.

Laila nodded and sat down in a rocking chair with the baby, "Go look at that picture," she said gesturing to a photograph that was set on a chest of drawers.

Matty walked over and picked it up with shaking hands. There was a woman and a man in the picture. The woman was being pushed by the man out of the hospital with a child in her arms. They were all smiling.

He studied the woman in the picture. He looked back and forth between her and Laila. They had the same blue eyes. Their hair was the same shade of brown. The pink lips and gentle smile were the same too. Laila was the woman in the picture.

Then, he looked in the mirror and he recognized himself as the man in the photograph. Laila was right. They were parents.

Silently, he turned to Laila and showed her the picture.

"I guess we made up," she said, trying to lighten the mood.

Matty smirked as he put the picture back. "Yeah, we must have."

All of a sudden, Matty and Laila heard a light knock on the nursery door.

"Should we open it?" Matty asked nervously.

"You can. I'm holding the baby," Laila said.

Matty opened the door slightly. At first, he thought there was no one there. Then, he looked down. In front of him was another kid. He was in a set of footie pajamas and he was holding a teddy bear. Matty thought he was probably two.

"Daddy," the kid smiled reaching his arms up to be held.

Instinctually, Matty picked him up. "Hey, buddy," he said walking back into the nursery.

The boy rested his head in the crook of his father's neck.

"There's another one…" Laila said emotionless because she didn't know which emotion to feel.

"A boy and girl," Matty said as if he needed to hear it spoken out loud to believe it.

Laila closed her eyes and focused on steadying her breathing. It was a lot to take in all at once. She and Matty were married in this escape and they had two children who didn't like to sleep.

"Matty, what if this became our life?" Laila asked, quietly as she put the sleeping baby back into her crib.

"I think," Matty said as he rubbed the back of the tot in his arms. "I would be happy. Like for real."

Laila cracked her knuckles. She didn't know if she would feel the same way. Maybe Matty would grow up and change and become a better communicator, but right now Matty was too difficult for Laila to understand. Sure, he was captivating, but that didn't make him kind to her and that didn't make him right for her.

"Can I hold him?" Laila asked, putting a hand on Matty's. They were sitting on the floor now and admiring their son who was falling back to sleep like his sister.

"Of course," Matty whispered before passing the boy carefully over to Laila.

Laila ran her hands through his dark, thick, curly hair and kissed his forehead. He smiled up at her and Laila noticed that he had deep brown eyes just like Matty.

"It's so amazing, isn't it? I mean they're so amazing," Matty marveled.

"They are both perfect. The most beautiful children I've ever seen," Laila said, and she wasn't lying. That's truly how she felt.

"Things work out so wonderfully," Matty mused.

"Hmmm.... I know I said I wouldn't bring this up but even though things seem like they're good for us in the future doesn't mean things are good between us right now. In case you've forgotten, we're still technically eighteen and we haven't talked for months."

Laila's words made Matty's face turn red. He didn't like how she was ruining the moment.

"Alright, I'm sorry, okay!" he scream-whispered.

"Me too," Laila said disappointedly.

"I think we could be forever if we try," Matty said with an air of melancholy. He leaned over and brushed the hair out of his sleeping son's face while Laila held onto the sweet boy a little tighter.

Laila breathed deeply through her nose and out from her mouth. "Let's find his bedroom and put him down for now. We can think about forever later."

Matty shook his head in frustration, but he didn't say anything. He stood up and slowly lifted the toddler from Laila's chest and carried him like a baby down the hall. Laila followed Matty and she opened a few doors until they found a room painted like the rainforest with a bed that had rails.

Matty laid the child down with his head gently resting on his Mickey Mouse pillow. Laila covered him with a blanket and they both kissed him on the cheek goodnight before walking out of the room and turning off the light.

"This is our house," Matty said again as if he couldn't believe it, "Let's go check it out."

Laila and Matty looked around the modest single-family home. On the top floor, there were three bedrooms and two bathrooms. Pictures of their little family covered the walls and the furniture was colorful and fun.

The kitchen had teal cabinets and white countertops. There was a pile of dishes in the sink which made sense because both Laila and Matty hated household chores. The living room had a quaint fireplace and there were toy race cars on the floor. *Toy Story* was still playing on the television.

The den was Laila's favorite room though. Bookshelves lined the walls and there was a cozy red loveseat in the corner of the room. A vibrantly colored spiral rug covered the center of the hardwood floor. To the side was a tiny antique desk with the kind of chair you would find in an old-timey ice cream parlor.

"It's my cozy place to read," Laila said with awe.

"Our wishes are going to come true," Matty said as he scanned the shelves while Laila studied the room with admiration. "Look, it's a photo album," he exclaimed, sitting down on the loveseat.

Laila sat down next to him and stroked the shiny cover. She wondered what secrets were inside. "Are you sure you want to look at this?" she asked.

"Of course," Matty replied. "Don't you want to know what the future holds?"

"I don't know. I kind of like not knowing. It makes every day a bit of a surprise."

"Well, I'm going to look because I want to know that everything is going to be alright," Matty explained.

Laila hesitated. "This might be a mistake, but I'm too curious not to look."

Matty slowly flipped open the front cover and they started to experience their life one picture at a time.

The first pages were filled with pictures from their college years, parties, walks around campus, and trips to fun places. There were sweet moments of the triplets growing up, birthday parties, and holidays too.

After the photos of Matty and Laila graduating from their colleges, were photos of them going to bars in the city, traveling to Europe, and attending concerts and plays. Laila's heart swelled with joy. She was going to get to have the adventures she had been dreaming about!

Then, the family era began. First, with a picture of Matty proposing to Laila up in the forest by the spring followed by dozens of shots from their small beachside wedding. The pattern continued with pregnancy announcements and proof of first steps taken.

Both Matty and Laila were speechless by the time they reached the midway point of the photo album and discovered the second half was blank.

"I guess this is the page of the story we're on right now," Matty said.

"Yeah, I suppose so, in the escape at least," Laila agreed. "But we're not even in this book yet at all. We're still in our parents' books 'cause our graduation day is more for them than it is for us."

"We have a wonderful life," Matty beamed.

Laila didn't say anything. The people in the photographs did have a wonderful life, but somehow, she didn't feel like she was the mother and wife, and student in those pictures, not yet. Plus, the pictures were only snapshots of Mr. and Mrs. Matty Holt's best moments. Laila wondered about the moments that didn't make it into the album. What about the things they didn't want to be remembered by but wouldn't be able to forget?

"These people in the pictures. We think they have a wonderful life, but we don't know if they do or don't. And they could be us but we're not them. We're just pretending to be."

"I'm too tired to understand what you just said," Matty said, but not sarcastically just honestly.

"I think I'm ready to go back," Laila whispered.

"Already? We have all night," Matty pouted.

"I don't think there's anything left to do here," Laila said looking into Matty's eyes sadly while patting his hand gently.

"What do you mean? There's everything to do here. Laila, we can live here as a family. Forget everything back home and just be happy in this home with our little children. We can skip over all of the stress of college and growing up and enjoy being put-together adults," Matty pleaded.

"Wait- are you serious? You're saying you never want to leave this escape. You want to be a put-together adult. You have to learn to do that. You don't know the first thing about being a father. You don't know how to cook. You can barely take care of yourself. You won't even know where you're supposed to go to work on Monday," Laila told him rather firmly.

"Laila," Matty said softly while he sweetly brushed a strand of hair out of her face, "I'm sorry for the way I've treated you, for anytime I've treated you as less than the princess that you are. Can you please forgive me because I need you, Laila? You're the only person who makes me feel like I'm not alone."

"Thank you, Matty," Laila replied politely. "But I meant what I said. I told you I loved you and I meant it, but I also told you that I wasn't going to play games and this feels so much like a game."

Matty sighed dramatically in exasperation. "Please, I'm not going back. There's too much pain and trouble to deal with. This escape feels good and safe. It feels like where we're meant to be."

"And maybe it is someday, but we have to be our real selves and experience life before we figure that out," Laila said as kindly as she could.

"Laila I can't go back. I lived without you and I can't do it again."

"No, Matty if you stay here. If you even can, don't you think it won't be. You'll know it's all a dream, a wish, and wouldn't that feel so fake. Don't you want to feel real?"

Matty thought about this for a moment. "No, I don't care about feeling real. I just want to feel okay. I don't care if it's fake."

"I'm going to wake you up once I'm back," Laila told him.

"I'm sorry. But I'm not ready to leave this escape," Matty whispered, shaking his head.

Laila rolled her eyes. "Okay. Well, then. Goodbye, but only for a second because you have to drive me home."

Matty just sat there while Laila closed her eyes and thought about growing up, going to college, and having adventures. It was a wonderful thought and in a blink of an eye, she found herself sitting in Matty's car in the dark feeling cold.

Laila reached over and immediately started shaking Matty's shoulder. She wanted to get him out of the escape and back into reality, but Matty wasn't responding. He wasn't doing anything at all. Laila pinched the skin on the palm of his hand hard, but that didn't work either.

"Matty!" she yelled, but Matty didn't hear her. Laila was starting to think he was right. Maybe you couldn't wake someone up from an escape. Maybe it had to be a choice to leave.

In desperation, Laila slapped Matty across the face with all the force she had. Matty didn't react at all.

Laila began to cry. She was stuck on the mountain at night when she should have been at her graduation celebration in a car with a completely unresponsive boy. How did this happen to her?

Then, Laila remembered to check his breathing and pulse like she had learned to do in first aid and CPR training. Much to the girl's relief Matty was still breathing and his heart was still beating, but she was still stuck.

For a moment, Laila just sat in the passenger's seat and bawled into her hands. She didn't know what else to do at that point, so she pulled out her phone and dialed 911. Something inside of her knew that Matty wasn't okay.

"911. What's your emergency?" the operator said.

"There's a boy with me and he's unresponsive," Laila explained as best as she could while practically hyperventilating. She continued to tell the dispatcher where they were and every detail about Matty's current state and the medication they had taken while an ambulance rushed up the mountain to meet them.

When the first responders came, Laila was separated from Matty immediately. While EMTs assessed Matty's state, a paramedic checked over Laila. He couldn't find anything wrong with her except that she was extremely anxious about her friend.

Tears streamed down Laila's face as she watched the ambulance rush away with Matty inside. The rest of the night was a blur to her, but she remembered her parents coming to pick her up and sobbing into her mother on the couch at a complete loss of words until she fell asleep and woke up the next morning.

Laila had fallen asleep on the couch in the living room and her mother had slept on the recliner to keep her company that night. Laila quietly tiptoed to the kitchen to check the time. It was only 6:00 a.m. She must have been too worried to sleep in, but the rest of her family still hadn't woken up.

She checked her phone, but there were no new notifications. Laila thought about texting Matty but knew he probably wouldn't reply. Instead, she walked outside and grabbed the local newspaper off the front porch.

Matty and Laila had made the front page. "Richardsville High Graduate Overdoses After Graduation" was the headline. Laila frantically skimmed the article for any new information on Matty.

According to the paper, Matty had taken more than the prescribed dosage of effugium, and he went into a coma as a result of hypoxic brain injury caused by the overdose.

Laila crashed onto the hardwood floor and sobbed loudly. She didn't care if it woke her parents up or even the triplets. This was the worst news she had ever heard in her life.

Her mother came and comforted her. To Laila's surprise, her mother didn't show any anger toward Laila for sneaking away with Matty and taking the effugium. She was supportive and empathetic entirely.

The family spent the rest of the day in agony waiting for news from Matty's parents.

"I want to go to the hospital and see him," Laila cried but she wasn't allowed.

At dinner, Mr. Holt called Laila's father and they talked for a long time. Laila's father took the phone call outside so that Laila wouldn't be able to overhear. Laila waited on the couch and stared at the television which was off. She was silent because she didn't have any tears left to cry.

Finally, her father came into the room and sat down next to his daughter. He wrapped his arm around her shoulder. "They're taking good care of him, but he still hasn't come out of the coma," Mr. Jennings told Laila.

Laila took a deep breath in. "They have to be able to do something else to help him," she protested.

"Trust me, darling, they are doing and are going to do everything they can. We must have faith," Laila's father assured her.

Laila just shook her head in despair and walked to her
bedroom. She wanted to take a nap and wake up from the horrible
nightmare she was living. But when she woke up there was no
escape from the painful reality of Matty being gone.

Every day for the rest of the summer went pretty much like
that for Laila and her family.

Sometimes Laila was allowed to go in and see Matty, but it
always made her sadder afterward because he just lay there in his
hospital bed hooked up to beeping machines in a room that smelled
like flowers but felt like death. Matty couldn't tell Laila that he
needed her anymore because Laila was never in the room with
Matty alone; she could never tell him how much she loved him.

A few weeks after the incident, Matty slipped into what the
doctors called a minimally conscious state. A doctor warned Laila
that Matty might never regain consciousness and if he did, he
would not be the same person he was before.

Laila tried not to believe the doctor's words. She thought
lies were supposed to feel bad, but this truth hurt much worse.

Often Laila wondered if Matty was still in the escape and if
so, what he was doing. She wondered if she was there too. She
wondered if Matty was in the escape if he could wish himself back
to reality if he wanted to or if he would be stuck there forever.

Sometimes Laila wanted to tell others about the escapes
and how Matty didn't want to go back that night. But she didn't
because it wouldn't have helped Matty regain consciousness and
everyone would have thought she was crazy.

Laila felt guilty somehow for everything that had
happened. She knew it wasn't her fault, but she wished she had
done something more or something different that would have
prevented Matty from overdosing.

August came and Laila was dreading leaving town for
school. She wanted to be near Matty and college didn't seem as
exciting as it had before.

"I think I'm going to be stuck here in this moment, in this
town, in this pain forever, and I don't care. It feels like it's where
I'm supposed to be," Laila told her grandmother as they sat one
afternoon sipping iced tea on the front porch.

"Why?" Grandma asked quietly.

Laila thought she was being insensitive. "Because of what happened. I can't move on. How could anyone move on from something like this?"

"Not everyone could, but you can, and you will."

"I don't want to," Laila whined.

"Laila don't ever forget him. That's not what moving on is about. Remember him. Remember what he meant to you, who he was, and what he taught you. Write it all down and take pictures of him in your mind. He changed you, Laila. I can see that. He's a part of you like no one else is. So, when you go out into the world and have experiences and meet new people and make change, he's going to be with you. He's going to be doing it all with you."

Laila started to choke up, but she held in her tears. "Thanks, Grandma," she said, biting her nails. "You're right as always and I am going to try. I'm really going to try to move on and remember him."

"I know you will, Laila," Grandma whispered, embracing her granddaughter's hand.

15 GROWN-UP

Laila grew up. She went to college and studied literature and creative writing. Laila never changed to fit in because she promised Matty that she wouldn't, but she did change in other ways.

She stopped writing poetry and sketching landscapes in class. Laila focused and paid attention because it became important to her to prepare herself to get a well-paying job in the future. Laila stopped spending so much time by herself as well. She went to parties and football games and concerts and she made a circle of friends.

Laila even opened an Instagram account to show the world everything she was doing and what a normal twenty-something she had become. Eventually, Laila decided it was time to date. She knew that Matty would always be her first love, and that was okay. Laila could love again and love differently with someone else.

She met a nice guy in graduate school. His name was Tom and he was a few years older and working for a publishing company. Tom and Laila dated for a couple of years and they fell in love. It wasn't a sweet, pure love like what Matty and Laila had. It was a twenty-first-century kind of love where you like the other person enough to have a family with them and you become each other's closest companions, but the real reason you stay with them after the attraction fades is the convenience. Tom and Laila loved each other, but they didn't know each other. It wasn't what Laila had dreamed of, but she accepted it because she was ready to settle down.

After traveling to all of the places Laila wanted to see and buying a home in the suburbs of Philadelphia, the couple tried for children. First, they had a girl who looked very similar to Laila's younger sister, Charlotte. They named the girl Eileen after Laila's grandmother. Two years after Eileen was born, Tom and Laila found out they were expecting a boy. They named the boy Matty after Laila's teenage friend who had been in a coma for the past ten years.

Tom provided for the family through his work as a publisher while Laila stayed home with their daughter and son. In her free time, she began to write down everything she had been thinking about for the last dozen years. She wanted to remember the story of Matty and Laila even though she went on to another chapter of her life and he stayed behind. Laila thought maybe someday she would be ready to share the truth of their friendship with the rest of the world, but it was still too soon for that. At least, she would have something to pass down to Eileen and little Matty if they would ever ask how her childhood ended.

One Tuesday afternoon in the summer, Laila decided to take her children then ages two and five for a drive to visit with their Aunt Lottie and Uncles Aaron and Ben who had just graduated high school. Laila wanted to visit with them before they went off to their separate colleges in the fall.

Laila passed the home that used to belong to her grandmother. She didn't dare to gaze at it as she drove by. That would be too painful.

Laila's Grandma had passed from natural causes of old age a few months before and it was still difficult for Laila every day. Grandma had been Laila's rock. Her whole life, Laila had wished for someone to talk to until after Matty went into his coma and Laila realized that her grandmother was her someone to talk to all along.

Laila's parents had cleared out the old cape cod and sold it to a young couple. Laila hoped the new owners were happy and taking care of the place that held so many of her most cherished memories.

Grandma's belongings were split amongst her children and grandchildren. Laila got to choose what she wanted first before her cousins and siblings, her father, and Aunt Claire decided because she had spent the most time with Grandma.

Laila felt horrible that she had not visited her grandmother during the final weeks before her death. It had been wintertime and Laila had been so overwhelmed with her little ones at home. Her child, Matty, who was just about to turn two at the time needed constant attention. He was always getting into pots and pans or spraying his father's shaving cream all over the bathroom.

Eileen who was nicknamed, Le-Le, was a handful as well. She could be sweet and play nicely with her little brother at times, but when it came to learning her alphabet or tidying up the playroom she could be impossibly stubborn.

Between snowstorms, sicknesses, and tantrums, Laila couldn't make the hour drive to Richardsville during the week. Tom didn't like spending his weekends in "that run-down town" and so Laila was out of luck.

Of course, Laila called home to her family every week when the kids were down for a nap and she could put the phone on speaker while folding laundry and it wasn't her fault that she hadn't been able to make it back home, but she would always feel bad anyway.

Aaron and Ben were out in the driveway of Laila's childhood home playing basketball when she parked the silver mini-van by the curb. Laila couldn't believe how they had grown before her eyes. She remembered when they were Eileen's age and all she wanted to do was get away from them. Now all three of the triplets were taller than her and smarter, she assumed.

Aaron and Ben helped Laila get the children out of their car seats. Matty and Eileen were over-the-moon to see them. They were good uncles always making it a point to sit on the floor and play dolls or cars or blocks with their niece and nephew.

On Christmas a few years prior, Laila complimented Ben on keeping Eileen entertained with piggy-back rides and hide-and-seek while Tom and a very pregnant Laila enjoyed eating dinner with the adults. Tom asked Aaron who was sitting across from him at the table who had taught them to be so good with kids because the men in Tom's family weren't like that.

"Well, Laila was always such a kind big sister and she had a friend, you know, Matty who always treated us like brothers and sisters when he would come over to the house," Aaron explained awkwardly but honestly. Suddenly, the room grew quiet because Matty's name wasn't mentioned often.

People didn't talk about Matty much a few years after the incident. It was one of those wounds time didn't heal. Maybe if Matty had died it would have been different. They might have been able to talk about him freely and remember him happily, but he hadn't died yet. He was still breathing. He was alive technically, but only as alive to them as a tree or a plant. That was the terrible reality everyone in the town lived with.

"Well, I'm glad our kids have such great uncles," Tom nodded while patting Laila's knee.

Laila was looking down at her plate. Thinking of Matty on Christmas was not something Laila could do without crying. "I think I need to use the bathroom for a moment," Laila mumbled quietly walking away from the table.

But she didn't go to the bathroom. She went up to her old bedroom. It had changed a little, but not a lot. The bed had a new comforter. The dresser had become a storage unit for Charlotte's extra clothes and the closet was now a museum filled with artifacts from Laila's childhood.

The paint was the same light blue as it had always been. The hardwood floor was covered with a bright, yellow rug that Laila had picked out for her sixteenth birthday. Posters of the Beatles still hung on the walls. A list titled "Laila's Greatest Dreams" written in black marker on flowery stationery hung by the mirror. She had written it when she started high school. Laila felt sad when she realized she penned it over half her lifetime ago.

She rummaged through her old desk drawers until she found a pen that wrote. The only one that wrote was one with lime green-colored ink, but it would do. Laila pulled the list from the wall and grabbed her high school yearbook from the shelf.

Laila sat down on the bed and sighed. She closed her eyes and rubbed her baby bump over the holiday sweater she was wearing. The little boy inside of her had just kicked hard. She smiled because that meant the baby was healthy.

Laila placed the list on her yearbook on her lap and began reading it from the top.

1. Become an author who inspires the world

Laila shook her head and chuckled cynically. She had been too ambitious, she thought. Laila crossed the words out with the bright ink. She didn't believe it would ever happen.

2. Travel the world

Laila circled it and added a heart. She had traveled the world and it had been a good stage of her life with Tom.

3. Find someone to talk to

She circled that one for Grandma.

4. Go to a concert

Laila drew a big circle around that one. The summer after she graduated high school, she went to her first concert. It was not at all like how she had imagined her first concert would be like.

Matty's mother called her in July and told Laila that Matty had purchased two tickets to Taylor Swift's *Reputation Stadium Tour* concert at Lincoln Financial Field. Mrs. Holt didn't know what to do with the tickets, so she gave them to Laila to do whatever she pleased with them.

Laila wanted to go for Matty, so she did, but she didn't have any friends to ask to go with her. She ended up taking her own mother. It was more fun than Laila had expected. She took a lot of pictures and put them in an album. Laila planned on giving them to Matty if he ever woke up.

5. Spend the night in the Magic Kingdom

Laila crossed that out. It was illegal and didn't sound fun anymore.

6. Meet the president

That hadn't happened, but presidents weren't cool like Barack Obama anymore, so she drew a sharp line through number six.

7. To know and be known

Laila hesitated, but in heart, she knew that she had. Laila knew Matty and Matty knew Laila. She circled it. Laila kissed the words briefly. She felt silly doing it, but she wanted to, so she did.

Laila got up and hung the list backup in its spot. Then, she picked up the small framed photo that was sitting on her dresser. It was a picture of Matty as you might have guessed. Laila took it on their day off. Matty was swinging up and down on the swings in the park. He had a big grin on his face. Laila remembered what it felt like to feel invincible. She kissed the photo through the glass gently as she recalled the sweet memory. This time the mother didn't feel silly. She felt brave.

Then, Laila glanced down at her fitness watch. She had better get downstairs before her mother started to worry. She had already taken too long. But before she went, she grabbed the photo in its frame and put it into her purse.

Laila returned to the kitchen to see her husband playing cards with her sister and her father showing her daughter how to make the Christmas train go.

"Are you okay, baby?" Laila's mother asked as she handed her a cup of tea and wrapped her arm around her shoulder.

"Yeah," Laila nodded.

"Are you sure? It looks like you've just woken up from a dream." Laila's mother was concerned, of course, because Laila was so far along in her pregnancy.

"I did, but I woke up to an even better one," Laila smiled.

Laila's mother was used to Laila saying strange, philosophical things like that. Laila had been doing it since she was a little girl.

"I'm glad," Laila's mother said as she wrapped her arms around her daughter. And then, Laila's mother whispered something into Laila's ear that made their bond stronger than it had ever been, "You don't have to love him any less because you found a good man who can hold you at night."

Laila was left speechless. Somehow her mother knew just the right words to tell her. "Thanks, Mom," Laila whispered back.

On this summer's day though, Laila wasn't thinking of Matty at all. That is to say, she wasn't thinking of her friend Matty Alexander Holt. She was, however, thinking of her toddler, Matty Thomas Stewart.

As Aaron and Benjamin took Laila's children to the backyard to play games in the treehouse, Laila went inside to visit with her mother and sister.

"Laila," Charlotte cried as she wrapped her arms around her older sister.

"Lottie! How's the packing going?" Laila asked.

"Good," Charlotte told her. "Dad just has to pick up a mini-fridge for me. Aaron and Ben haven't started at all, though."

"Oh, well, they get that from me," Laila said.

Laila's mother came down, then and the three women gossiped and laughed in the kitchen for a while until the boys and little Eileen came in from the hot sun for lemonade and a snack.

Laila felt happy and at peace. She was grateful to have Richardsville to escape to when things got to be mundane or a little too much at home.

Eileen and Matty were starting to yawn, so Mrs. Jennings took them up to her bedroom where she would read picture books to them until they fell asleep for a short catnap.

Laila suggested to her siblings that they go on a walk. They groaned at this because it was hot in the afternoon but agreed anyway. So, all four of the Jennings children went on their way. Even though they were grown they all still had a bit of that adventurous, child-like, free spirit left in them.

Laila advised her siblings as she felt it was her sisterly duty to do before they started college. She told them to remember to work hard, to make good friends and memories, and to always keep those parts of them that made them each unique.

Charlotte and Aaron thought their sister's speech was sweet because they were both the sentimental type. Ben rolled his eyes. He knew Laila had good intentions but found her monologue a little cheesy.

"I'm going to miss you guys," Charlotte said as they walked. Laila intertwined her hand with her sister's and gave it a reassuring squeeze.

"Tom and I and the kids will visit you at State," Laila promised.

"Yeah, but Ben and Aaron will be off in New York and I'll barely get to see them," Charlotte lamented. She was always the most expressive with her emotions and was inclined to be a little dramatic.

"Oh, come on, Lottie," Ben said giving her a playful push on the back, "we won't even be as far as Justin across the state in Pittsburgh."

Aaron smirked and Ben winked at his brother after noticing that Aaron liked his tease. "Shut up, Ben!" Charlotte whined, reminding Laila of when she was a pre-teen.

"Who's Justin?" Laila blurted out immediately her girlish instinct kicking in.

"Oh, he's only the-" Aaron started but was hushed by his older sister.

"I didn't ask you, Aaron. I asked Lottie, but since you want to talk let's talk about Camilla. Mom mentioned her on the phone to-"

"Stop, alright. I won't tease. I get it," Aaron protested blushing.

This time Charlotte and Laila were the ones smirking while Ben erupted with laughter. Laila was going to give some words of wisdom on finding love, but she thought better of it. Love can't be taught. It has to be learned through experience, through adventure, through exploration, through trial and error, through pure bliss, and painful memories.

The four walked in silence for a moment. They were all very thoughtful people so quiet moments were very comfortable for them and not awkward at all. Eventually, they reached the block by the park.

"Hey," Ben piped up. "Let's make a memory."

Laila grinned from ear-to-ear because it was just the type of thing she would have said when she was his age.

"Let's take off our shoes and walk through the creek," he suggested. Everyone liked the idea and that's what they did.

The water was warm, a couple of feet deep, and clear. They acted half their age and picked up the shiniest rocks to keep in their pockets. Ben tried to tease Charlotte by picking up a crayfish and getting nearer and nearer to her until she shrieked.

They had a good time until about twenty minutes into their journey Ben's phone rang. It was their mother, but he ignored it because he didn't want the fun to end. Then, Aaron's phone rang, and he picked it up.

"What is it, Mom?" Aaron asked.

"Can you guys come home?" Mrs. Jennings' asked with concern in her voice.

"Yeah, I guess so. Is everything okay? Are the kids awake?"

"Everything's fine. There's just something I need to tell all of you guys and not over the phone."

Aaron rolled his eyes. He didn't want to come home yet. "Alright, we're on our way, then. I guess."

"Guys, we got to head back. Mom has something to tell us and, it can't wait," Aaron told his siblings sarcastically.

Ben groaned, but they all trudged home anyway.

"What was the big news that just couldn't wait?" Charlotte asked as they kicked off their shoes by the front porch and entered the door.

Their mother had a strange expression and none of her children could exactly tell how she was feeling. She looked over at Laila, took her hands into her own, and smiled, "Matty's awake," she said.

"What?" Laila muttered.

Laila's mother nodded her head. "It's in the news. It's everywhere. His mother called me. He's in rough shape, but he's alive and he's aware."

Laila sat down on the staircase and cried happy tears while her little sister rubbed her back. Everyone was smiling. It was a miracle they never expected.

"Can he talk?" Laila asked.

"Short sentences and phrases," her mother replied, "but his voice is shaky and he's very confused."

Laila didn't care about how well Matty could speak. The good news she received was more than she could have ever asked or hoped for.

Just then, little Eileen came stumbling down the stairs from her nap. "Why are you crying, Mommy?" she asked.

"Oh," Laila said, picking up her baby in her arms and landing kisses all over her head, "Mommy's happy. Her friend was very sick, but now he's better.

16 MIRACLE

The doctors and nurses and the entire scientific community were shocked at Matty's awakening. Everyone pretty much assumed he was just going to die one day with his feeding tube in and no last words to say.

When Laila went to see Matty on that first day, the cameras were there, and people were asking her questions. It was a big deal to the world, to the town, but most of all to those who loved Matty all along.

Matty's face lit up when he saw Laila for the first time. She ran over and hugged the frail man and told him how much she missed him, but all Matty could say was her name, so he repeated it over and over. It made Laila very happy to hear him say her name.

Laila wanted to spend as much time as she could with Matty, but she couldn't because she had a life away from Richardsville and kids to take care of and a house to manage. She was grateful to Tom though who offered to take care of the children on the weekends so Laila could go back to Richardsville and visit with Matty.

Slowly, but surely Matty improved. It seemed that each week Laila came to see him there was something new and exciting for him to share. First, it was relearning to talk with the right pronunciations. Then, it was transitioning to solid foods and eventually feeding himself with a spoon. With the help of therapists, he was able to do most basic tasks albeit slower than average by the end of twelve months. He was still unable to walk, but there was hope for him to relearn that someday too.

Matty and Laila never talked about any of the hurt or any of the joy either. For once, they just focused on the now, on Matty recovering and on getting him caught up to speed with the world. A lot had happened in the last decade. Neither ever mentioned escaping or the effugium. Laila wondered if Matty even remembered it.

Then, one September day, over a year since the day Laila had received the happy news, she found out how well Matty did remember.

Laila took Matty outside for a walk around Richardsville that afternoon. The air was changing into fall, but the sun was still warm and bright like summer.

"Remember those wishes we made here?" Matty asked suddenly as Laila pushed him around the path in the park.

"Yeah," Laila replied quietly rerunning the events through her head.

"Did they come true for you?"

"I think so. I'm happy now," Laila reflected.

"Me too. I'm glad I came back," Matty admitted.

"So," Laila implored in a soft voice so as not to be overheard, "You were really in that escape for twelve years and then you just wished yourself back like we always did."

"Yes," Matty told her ashamedly, "I thought you knew that."

"I didn't know, not with any certainty. Matty you left me. How could you do that? You made me live without you for so long." Laila felt abandoned and rejected.

"I needed you so badly in my life. I couldn't ever risk not having you, so I sacrificed having the real you," Matty explained on the verge of tears. Laila didn't want to make him upset, but she was angry and confused thinking about the many years they lost together, all of the pictures in the photo album that were never taken.

"I loved you, Matty," she told him looking into his never-changing, mystical brown eyes. She had sat down on a park bench and placed him in his wheelchair beside her.

"I know, but I was eighteen and I didn't know what love was. I only knew what hurt felt like."

"That's a stupid excuse," Laila said biting down on her lip so she wouldn't cry.

"I know I love you now," Matty whispered sincerely.

"I love you, but you know I'm married now, and I have the two most wonderful, beautiful children. It's too late for a second chance, Matty," Laila explained.

"Is it too late to kiss you just once?" Matty asked longingly.

"Don't ever say something like that again," Laila scolded, turning her face away from him.

"Well, what do you have to say, then? Should I just disappear out of your life forever?"

"No, I thought you learned," Laila became gentle again, her love overpowering the frustration she felt.

"Then what do you say, Laila. Please, I need hope," Matty pleaded.

"I say we have a lot of work to do."

Escape

Struggling with substance abuse or drug misuse? Know a friend who needs help? Visit https://teenchallengeusa.org for information on how to find support.

Made in the USA
Middletown, DE
27 January 2021